KINGS OF THE R

Saturday was pretty slow and I lounged around the house trying to be helpful in the morning and when that didn't work I went and bought myself a Bell, that being a helmet, and then rode around for a couple of hours having a fine time. But soon I got to wish that I could share it with someone so I called up everybody that I knew from school – but all the girls were out, or were studying, or were still at school, or I wasn't allowed to talk with them.

So I rode around some more and then I got the fine idea of riding down to Brighton . . . It was about five in the evening and it was beautiful, with the sun still shining strong and the sky all blue and not much traffic on the road and I rode out through Streatham and Croydon and just after Purley I joined up with a gang of Angels on a run and I rode with them down the motorway . . . It was a sight with the pack of us thundering down the motorway and it made me laugh watching the faces of the car drivers as we swept by.

G.O.B.
Goods on Board

SIMON MAYLE

SPHERE BOOKS LIMITED
London and Sydney

First published in Great Britain by
Sphere Books Ltd, 1986
30–32 Gray's Inn Road, London WC1X 8JL
Copyright © Simon Mayle, 1986

**TRADE
MARK**

Set in 10/12pt Compugraphic English

Printed and bound in Great Britain by
Cox & Wyman Ltd, Reading

1

To most fellows this business of expulsion was not something to be taken too seriously. But to mothers, all of them I reckon, expulsion was certainly an evil and rotten crime, even if it was an accident of sorts.

I was thinking these things on the way back from what must have been my fifth school in three years, and I was looking out the window of the cab (I always took cabs home after expulsion), and I reckon I was probably doing an awful lot of trembling too, for old mumma could be plenty fierce when she wanted to be.

When we pulled up to the curb outside our home, she was standing there, on the top step, all moody gloom and wearing black. I paid the cab and we went inside.

As I expected we did not talk for the first ten minutes or so. We didn't say 'Hallo', we didn't kiss, shake hands, look each other in the eye, discuss the weather – nothing. We did what we always did on those special occasions: the suitcases were parked in the hall of our ground-floor flat; I was led through to the kitchen; I was instructed to sit on one of the wooden benches at the pine table; and old mumma made the tea. It was like that every time.

I bit my nails.

'Here,' mother said, passing me a steaming mug. I took the mug and she sat down on the bench opposite, saying nothing. I started fidgeting and still nothing was said. We sipped tea and I picked at my palms. I don't mind telling you I was nervous then. She was a champion at making a boy nervous. Eventually she asked me why I did it and I

1

couldn't tell her because I didn't have too much of an idea myself. So I muttered something and took cover.

My mother suffers from a terrible temper – I think it is the Irish in her – and when she starts she is a very difficult lady to stop. Impossible, some would say (my dad in particular). I watched her boil over, always ready to duck underneath a vicious left that she had a habit of unleashing in moments of extreme frustration, always ready to run if the situation degenerated and she started to become all rabid. I heard things like this:

'How can you do this to us, James [that's my name] after all we've done for you? After all the sacrifices and hard work and tears that have been invested [a key word] in your past to enable you to travel life's many rocky roads and reap the rewards that only a good education can offer . . . Don't you realise that in order to get on in this world, one must have *qualifications*, that in order to strive, to achieve *great* things one must have a solid educational background . . .' etc., etc.

Well, this sort of jabber went on for ten minutes or so. Enough time to strip every nail from my finger, pick every loose bogey in my nose, and pray to the good Lord that something would interrupt this all-righteous soliloquy. I think he must have been listening because just at the point where I was about to be banned (I think for life) from ever doing anything, the telephone rang.

Now, due to my mother's weighty social commitments the telephone is enshrined in a reverential position in the hall (underneath my mother's portrait) and treated like a god. When it rings, it demands to be answered. It is like a holy summons, normally with an invitation for lunch or dinner or the theatre or some gala opening or ball or whatever, and to leave it ringing is sacrilege.

Inside, I smiled. Mother fled.

It was Lucy with an invitation for lunch to meet some 'super' people. To me and my little brother she was known as Juicy Lucy because of her size and salivating habits. She was a real case and she loved Pook. She liked to fondle him, openly.

'Does the diddywithims like to be tickled then?' she'd say. (That was her excuse.)

'No, get lost Lucy,' my little brother would say. But it never did any good. She'd maul him, thrusting his poor little head into her ample bosom, cooing like some bloated and rancid pigeon. 'Come to Auntie Lucy,' she'd coo; 'just want a teency weency cuddle, you gorgeous little creature.'

Now don't get me wrong, I really like women, but this thirteen-stone pervert hofferlump was too much. Though, on that day, Miss Lucy sprouted the wings of an angel, saving my poor soul and indeed my little ears from a Hellfire of a roasting.

After twenty minutes on the phone (a short conversation) I heard mother's footsteps return on the creaky wooden floorboards of the hall. Her small quick steps were a sure sign that our little talk was soon to be concluded.

It was, and I was to wait in for my father's return from the office so that he 'could pull the wind out of your sails'. Then, after one final 'How could you do this to us?' gaze, she left.

As you can see, her conversation is sprinkled with all sorts of champion metaphorical clichés and that last one about the wind and the sails had me puzzled for a bit. I was tempted to question it – after all, there is no wind that I know of that has handles – but questioning such things only invites an earful.

I should now tell you about our glorious flat, about how long we have lived there, about who lives there, what it looks like and all that other rubbish – but I won't. I'll tell you about my room. It is certainly the best room in the flat, armed with a lock to keep out the fossils and graced with a window for hasty escapes up the drainpipe, in cases of emergency. This window was the second door to the flat. It provided access to the roof, via the drainpipe and Mrs Arnold-Harrison's window box, and then from the roof there were stairs leading down to Pavillion Road. A valuable asset.

The room was a mess when I walked in: everything was in its place; the beds were made, the posters were straight on the wall, the carpet was hoovered, it even smelt clean. It took me twenty minutes of hard labour to organise the room so that it had some reasonable semblance of its former glory. I pulled out my socks, slung them on the floor, emptied the contents of the suitcase on one of the beds, unstraightened a few posters, closed the window, opened all the cupboard doors, got out all my dirty magazines and then when I was satisfied that things were looking better, I had a snooze.

Pook woke me, pouncing on me like a pussy-cat. He does that all the time.

'How are you, Pook?' I said.

He laughed. 'You got kicked out again?'

'No, half-term.'

'Liar.'

He was sitting on the bed opposite, all five feet and two and a half inches of him. He had the dog with him. He's a great brother, though just a little too popular with the ladies. Every girl I ever brought home would invariably hug him and kiss him and say how sweet he was and of course he could make them laugh which loosened everything up a little and helped me out no end, as I was always nervous. At the age of eleven I'd say he had felt more chests in his life than most men would think of in a lifetime. Sometimes my girlfriends would drop by the flat just to see old Pook. Fortunately, he was open to bribery: a Mars and two packets of Opal Fruits would see him out the door leaving me in the company of my loved one.

'What happened this time? Did you swear at anybody? Did you? How 'bout hit someone? Did you thwack a teacher? Did you? Well did you?'

I told him I didn't want to talk about it, it made me too upset and as he wasn't yet familiar with the emotive forces that are at work in the body after such a traumatic event it would be better if we talked about something else. Like Marie, my mother's pretty French helper. He didn't want to talk about her as she was the culprit responsible for keeping his room tidy, and as a consequence some rotten stick of sherbert that had been hidden and saved for a very special occasion had gone missing.

'Who told you?' I said.

'Mum.'

'Is she back?'

'With Lucy and some other people. I think she's drunk.'

'Are they going out this evening?'

'She said they might go to the theatre if they could get Marie to babysit.'

'What's wrong with me?' I said. And of course the answer was simple: I was not responsible enough to be allowed to look after my little brother on my own. I needed assistance. I needed assistance to accomplish the simple task of looking after myself. And Marie's assistance was a joyful assistance for it would not be false to say that I harboured secret and passionate visions of the two of us sharing an idyllic happiness in a far-away land. I was very naive then, but did she have big tits. They were something.

'Is dad home?' I asked.

'Not . . .' And then the doorbell rang.

Instantly I despatched my trusty brother with strict instructions (lies) of my whereabouts. As it was six thirty in the evening it could only be my poor tired dad that was ringing the bell at this hour.

5

The ruse failed and within three minutes I heard the fearful and ponderous step of my father on the floor-boards of the hall.

I hid.

'James?' he said in that pompous voice of his as the bedroom door opened slowly. I did not answer. We had played this game many times in the past and I was well acquainted with the fact that old fossils aren't too fond of bending. Hence the choice of hiding place – in the dark-ness under the bed. In summers past, Pook and I had made a regular wage from simply following my granny about her house during our stay there, picking up all the things that she dropped or knocked over.

He found me within five minutes.

'How are you Dad?' said I, smiling and crawling out from my lair. 'Good to see you looking so well.'

Father did not seem too happy.

He didn't reply. He made me feel uneasy with a gaze that he used, one that was reserved for the most weighty matters. I looked up at the ceiling, I looked at the walls, I even untied and tied my shoelaces, waiting for him to start.

'James, James, James, James, James,' he said over and over. 'What *are* we going to do with you?'

He let out an enormous sigh, shifted his position and waited. I looked at him and tried to assume a meek, mod-est and shamed look.

'Well, to tell you the truth, Dad, I don't rightly know.'

This was probably the only truthful statement I made throughout our little talk. I promised him that it wouldn't happen again; that I was indeed very sorry; that in the future I would not mix with the 'bad' elements in the school etc., etc. Then we discussed my future (it was not much of a discussion), the short- and long-term effects my expulsions were having on my mother (she came out in a terrible rash that had to be treated immediately by the most expensive dermatologists in Harley Street, and at the end of the quarter there was a significant rise in the telephone bill), and to top if off there was the question of what I should be doing with myself during the summer months.

There was a slight pause, then inspiration humped its evil way into the dirty part of the mind in the beautiful and curvy form of young Marie. I instantly set forth a proposal which under the circumstances I felt was quite admirable: I suggested that I should be sent abroad with young Marie as chaperone, interpreter and teacher. Unfortunately he didn't think this was a particularly good idea. He mentioned something about me not deserving it. Of course I argued with great enthusiasm. I pointed out that I had not yet passed any of my French exams in all of my seventeen years, and that if I were to I would be out of his hair for the summer (a sore point with him considering he does not have much), and that by the time I returned to England I would undoubtedly be fluent in the language. . . .

'No, James, no. I have an idea of what would be best and it certainly does not entail a trip to foreign parts, no.' The old man shook his head and smiled.

'Marie's parts aren't foreign, Dad.'

'What did you say, boy?'

'Nothing, Dad.'

There was an awkward pause and then he dropped the bomb. 'I think', he said, 'it would be a jolly good thing if you spent this summer working, don't you?'

'Working?'

'Yes!' he said triumphantly.

'No!'

'But you *must*, James.'

I retreated into a state of shock, unable to answer. Work? Was the man a loony? After five gruelling weeks in a learning establishment, a boy needs a rest. A five-month rest to be precise. I wasn't going to work if I could possibly avoid it. But I did not want to argue – I harboured vicious thoughts of a beating to be handed out by my dear old Dad and his faithful steel ruler.

'You're right; it's a great idea, a real cracker. I'll get onto it in the morning, first thing. Yes sir!' I said.

The old man smiled his best wrinkly smile, mumbled something about thinking I'd see it his way, and left.

That night I suffered the worst nightmares I would remember in all my years.

2

The following morning old Mother dear woke me much earlier than I had wished. She stomped into the room, threw open the curtains and shrieked, 'Jayy-yames. Up, up, up. Breakfast's ready! Come on!'

This was another horrible habit that the lady had adopted after I had these small misunderstandings with the academic establishment. Mother would wake me, kick me out of the bed, force food inside me and then load me with errands to keep me occupied in my day and out of trouble's reach.

As I said nothing in reply, she tried again, only this time she went up an octave. This had a more penetrating effect on the eardrums.

I slipped one eye out from underneath the covers and saw her silhouetted against the morning light. From the angle at which I lay, she looked much taller and broader than usual. Her long brown hair hung straight on her face framing the blue eyes, the large nose, the archer's bow mouth and the square chin. Her head was set forward slightly and her hands rested firmly on her hips. She struck up an imposing figure.

I retreated under the covers.

'Oh no you don't, you little devil! Up you get. I believe your father has already instructed you on what you must do today. Isn't that so?'

'No. He was only joking, he didn't mean it, Mum. Honest,' said I, clearing the sleep dust from the weary eyeballs.

She tried the old trick of ripping the blankets from the bed; but I foiled the attempt.

'James' she said. 'If you don't get up right this instant your food will be cold and spoiled and I will have to throw it away. So please, *get* up, young man!'

Mother was not a good cook. She brought life to her food but it wasn't the sort of life a person would like to meet at the table unarmed. I tried to pass this one.

'All right, Mother, I'll be right there. You go on back to the kitchen, and I'll follow you when I've dressed.'

'No James, I know your tricks and I'm not leaving here until you leave that bed of yours.'

This could have been a highly embarrassing situation. I was already up (in a manner of speaking) and it was my upness that concerned me. If I had left my bed it would have concerned her too. So I pleaded that I was naked, shy and unwilling to show her me plonker. She left.

Pook was sitting at the breakfast table when I walked in.

'Morning Pook!' I said and I sat down on the bench opposite, where a place was laid. I poured some Frosties in a bowl and on top, some milk. Pook read his comic in silence. Mother was standing in the far corner next to this important-looking cooker we had just had installed. It did just about everything except cook the food. This was a shame because as I said, Mother couldn't cook to save her life. God knows what she thought she was doing to ours.

'Have you got the papers today, Mum?'

'No, your father took them to work with him. Here.'

She put the plate down and it banged as it hit the surface. It was one of those white plates that the French use, as she had recently discovered French Style. (She thought it 'super' and 'fun'.)

On it lay my breakfast, not a sight for the squeamish.

'Eat,' she instructed. 'You'll need all your strength today, if you're to find a job.'

'What about errands? Haven't you got any of them you want run? Huh? I could do errands today and maybe find a job tomorrow.' I put on my most endearing face, and as a gesture of goodwill I ate a mouthful.

'No, no, I can't think of anything you can do for me,' she said. 'There are some small jobbies to be done, but I am perfectly capable of doing them myself. If you wish to stay on the right side of your father, dear, and not make him peeved, then come home this evening with news of a job.'

'That's easier said than done. Where do I look?' said I, wrestling with a sausage.

'I don't know,' she replied. One of the sausages she was cooking for Pook flamed. 'Why don't you ring your father and see if he can slot you into a job on the floor at the Stock Exchange? Or perhaps I could ring Nigel and ask him if you could possibly work in his stables –'

'Mum, the sausages.' Pook instructed.

'What?'

'Could I have them cooked, please. Not cremated.'

'Oh *sorry*, darling!'

With the spatula in her right hand and the grill in her left, Mum pulled the sausages out and battered them on their backs with the spatula until the flame had died and they had split their skins oozing meat and fat on the grill tray.

'No,' I said. 'I don't fancy any of them much.'

'Why not? They'd be simply wonderful jobs to have if you could get in. You'd learn stacks and you'd meet all the right people. It would be frightfully useful for you in later life, you know. Very useful indeed!'

'No thanks.'

'Well I think you are a fool James, and I don't think you realise how difficult it is to find a job.'

'Right.'

'What *are* you going to do?'

'I'll look around.'

'You can't just look around, James. Jobs don't grow on

11

trees, you know. There are millions of unemployed out there, just millions, and most of them would give their right arm for the opportunity. Their *right arm*, James.'

She paused to let the effect of the words sink in. I looked at Pook. He rolled his eyes.

'So, James?'

'So what?'

'So what are you going to do?'

'I told you, I'll look around.'

'What!' she screamed. I got up from the table and went to my room, her voice echoed down the corridor behind me.

'James? Jay-yames? Come here when I'm speaking to you. D'you hear me? James?'

3

It was cold and windy and overcast when I finally slipped out of the building with my push-bike. Mother dear was still nagging about work and the state of the nation as I left. I think I might have had a headache. Her nagging always gave me headaches. From the road I could see her small figure standing by the window. Her mouth was moving and she was saying all sorts of things of which I could hear nothing. She was still nagging. Of course, I was nodding my head in complete agreement with her, smiling like a champion all the time, and when I was finally ready to peddle off I gave her the A.O.K. and thumbs up sign. Yes mother, I shall certainly be home with news of work.

Once out of visual range I slackened off the enthusiasm with the peddles and started to ponder the dilemma of where I was to spend the rest of the day. As I had absolutely no intention of finding a job, I tried thinking of old friends that I could visit and there were, unfortunately, none. Everybody was still at school. But that was a comforting thought – they were, most likely, studying. Ha ha.

I reasoned that if I could come home each evening desolate, depressed, exhausted but still doggedly determined to find a job, their enthusiasm for me being employed might diminish and eventually disappear. But then there was always the vicious threat of that old tosser Nigel; or the Stock Exchange. To get out from being snared by either of those two was going to require some wily ways. These were the things I thought about as I pedalled up Sloane Street.

Ten minutes passed of aimless cycling. I had travelled at least half a mile and having strenuously avoided exercise for all of my schooling, that half-mile was a punishing one. Now knackered, I sat on a bench at Hyde Park Corner.

I watched the cars, I ate chocolate and the tourists took it in turns to take pictures over by the big stone monument standing in the middle.

Then something wonderful happened. I was watching this old granny, whilst wrestling with a piece of toffee, and she was cycling hell for leather on her granny bicycle around the roundabout when this wanker of a cabdriver suddenly cut her up. She almost got pushed into the curb and could have fallen and broken something. She didn't though, she stayed upright and when she caught the cabbie at the light, for it was red and he had to stop, she smacked him one. Hit him right on the hooter. She was magnificent. I cheered for her and the cabbie fled, jumping the light. So I stayed in the square a little longer, half hoping to see something else before I cycled down to Victoria to play the arcades down there with the fifty pence I had in my pocket. And these horses came – there were about five of them – led by a fine looking woman, a little stout, wearing unnecessarily tight riding trousers of a creamy colour, a hat, and holding a whip. Behind her I saw two Arabs, and the others I couldn't see too well. They slowly came my way.

And all of a sudden, above the sound of the big buses and the diesel-engined cabs and the cars and the trucks, I heard a powerful motor howl. The sound came from Knightsbridge and it gave the effect that whatever it was, it was moving much faster than anything else. Some American tourists who had been studying the inscription on the stone wall behind me were also attracted and curious to discover what was making such a racket. Just over the car roofs in the distance, bent over backwards in the wind, I

saw an aerial. The man on the motor-cycle was flying
through the traffic, carving a sweet line through the buses
and the cabs and the cars, utilising all three lanes of the
busy road. Swooping from one lane to another and back. I
was watching him when the horns went off and when I
turned back to look at the roundabout a little man in a
blue Mini with a balding head had his window down and
was shouting filthy obscenities at the big woman. The big
woman raised her hand, just like they do in the cavalry.
Her troupe stopped. More horns.

She shouted at him: 'Run along little man!'

The little man didn't feel like running far and continued
to tell the lady what she should do with herself, how she
should do it, where it could be done, and with whom. He
thought about getting out of his car but fear got the better
of him when she raised her horse-whip. He quickly drove
off amidst more horn blowing and I think that was what
flustered him and caused him to stall. By this time the
motor-cycle man had travelled all the way along Knightsbridge and was now ready to attack the roundabout, but
his entrance path was blocked by the fool in the Mini.
When he hit the brakes, the sound was something terrible
– hideous squealing and rubber tearing as the motor-cycle
started a long fish-tailing slide.

I turned away.

When I turned back the motor-cycle had hit the car but
only as a glancing blow and now the bike was parked up by
the curb, in front of me.

'Did you see that?' said the motor-cycle man lifting his
visor.

'Most of it,' I said, getting up from my bench and walking across. The man took his helmet off. He hardly had
any hair and his face was as gaunt as any face I've ever
seen. We started talking, mostly him shouting, in fact,
about the lack of a rear right indicator and what action he,
the skinhead, was going to take on the driver of the Mini

(he was going to kill him). This was all said in a rush as he struggled to get his leather gauntlets off, as he propped the machine on the side stand, and as he ran into the road causing more cars to squeal and making me stand behind as principal witness. That poor Mini driver, he was quaking in his boots shooting nervous glances at the rapidly approaching leather figure, all boots and black leather. He was also trying to persuade the horsewoman to come to his assistance, but she did not want to know and spurred her horse on its way.

When the Mini-man had been marched over to me by the scruff of his collar, the tall, booted and leathered skinhead asked me, 'Whose fault was it?' I pointed at the poor wretch hanging by his shirt-collar.

'Too fucking right it's his fault. Look what you fucking done you fucking bastard,' said the skinhead.

We all assessed the damage.

'That fucking stall'll cost you thirty fucking quid *at least*, plus loss of fucking earnings, means I'm going to have to fucking charge you for the fucking time spent going to the fucking shops to buy a fucking replacement. I mean *Look* at it!'

And so it was and so too would be the little man with the hairy brows and no hair.

'I . . . I . . . ccan't pay you tthirty ppounds,' the little man stammered as he tried to loosen his collar, to allow air to travel to a face that was red and glowing. But the skinhead wouldn't loosen his grip and was adamant about the price. Then the Americans joined in.

'I don't think your bein' vehry fehr, young man,' drawled a deep southern accent belonging to a large and aggressive looking woman in a loud check suit.

'You what?' said the skinhead.

'It weren't his fault.'

'Who's asking your opinion, Topo?'

'I was watchin' you young man drivin' that devil possessed machine of yers and I coulda sworn an accident like this would have happened. You was jus' drivin' plum plain too fast and aah said to mah husban' aah said. . .'

'Piss off. Go on, on yer bike.'

'Now there ain't no cause for you to be rude, boy. Mah husban' Archie, he . . .'

The skinhead interrupted her, moving close so that his face was barely six inches away from hers. 'Shut . . . Up . . . You . . . Blithering . . . Idiot,' he said very slowly. Then he smiled. For a moment the skinhead had as my mother would say, 'pulled the wind from her sails'. But it was only for a minute.

'Aarchie, did you hear what that boy said to me? Well did ya?'

'Yes dear,' said Archie.

'Well? What' you goin' to do about it?'

Old Archie wasn't too sure; he turned his head away from the argument and looked meditatively up towards the grey sky. The wind had started to blow off the park and it rustled his short silver hair. 'Well dehr,' he said after a while, 'mebbe we should sorta leave these people sort their own problems out.'

'Spoken like a fucking general, mate. A right general,' the skinhead cooed, smiling.

'No, Aarchie,' the lady went on. 'As members of the Peoples Church of South Carolina, we have an obligation here. A moral obligation to save people from sinners. And Archie,' she said, turning from her husband to face the big booted gangly leather man, 'this man *is* a sinner!'

Good luck lady, I thought. She was a fine hen and looked most impressive with her jowls bloated and the fire in her eyes. But the skinhead looked plain mad. Demented even.

He smiled and said: 'How'd you like a slap round the chops?' Here is where I stepped in, explaining to them all the causes of the accident – the horsewoman, the Mini

17

and all the time being very careful to avoid the issue of the motor-cycle's speed, knowing that this skinhead had a pair of large and rather well-used looking knuckles. And to conclude, I suggested that the Americans should leave whilst still in full possession of their faculties and features.

Archie, being a born leader and a wise old soul, responded to the call immediately, placating his warmongering wife and leading the group away.

'Fag?' said the skinhead holding out an open pack of Number 6s.

'No thanks,' said I.

'So what's it going to be then?' said the skinhead. 'Cash or cheque, I don't mind which, I'm not a difficult man.' And with that said, he lit his cigarette.

'I don't have th-th-thirty pounds,' the little man replied meekly.

'Oh come, come,' said the skinhead. 'You jest. Every Mini driver in London has to have at least thirty pounds on their person when operating such a vehicle. It is a necessity.'

'It is?'

'Yeah 'coz bits always fall off Minis, don't they? I mean take that number plate for example. Look what happens if I give it a swift kick . . .'

The skinhead let go of the man's collar and ran up to the car and kicked it in the boot. The number plate dropped off. He brought it back to us. 'Now,' he continued, 'how much is one of these? Thirty quid at least, innit? Eh?'

The little man nodded.

'So what do you do about it?'

The little man didn't know.

'Well I'll tell you then, squire. You keep some *cash* on yer person in case of *accidents* and other such misdemeanors. So, the thing is, 'ave you or 'aven't you thirty pound? Because if you 'aven't, I might have to do a check on your Mini and see what else falls off. I mean, we can't have your driving around the place with bits falling off. It would be dangerous wouldn't it, eh?'

'I think I have got *some* money.'

'Oh, just remembered it 'ave you? That's good, I thought you might have some somewhere. You just needed a little surprise to jolt your memory.'

The little man and the skinhead went over to the car and soon the skinhead came back counting his money. The little man packed his number plate in his back seat and drove off, white-faced.

'What do you do?' I asked.

'I'm a mugger.'

'No, for work.'

He spat on the pavement and when he had finished counting his money he looked up and said, 'Despatch rider on the brmm brmm.'

'Oh.'

'What d'you do?'

'Nothing.'

'Unemployed?'

'Thankfully.'

The skinhead smiled. 'The idle rich, wot a fucking life. What's it like? Is it good? Eh?'

'Not bad. What about despatch riding? What's that like?'

'It's better than football. I get in a ruck every day on the road. Yesterday was my best day ever.'

'Why, did you make a lot of money?'

'Nah, had four rucks, two Cortina drivers, one cabbie and got pasted by a trucker. Fucking magic it were.'

Strange man, I was thinking.

'Well how much money do you make?'

'None of your business.'

When I asked him if he made over a hundred pounds, he scoffed at the suggestion and said that not even the worst riders in the company made less than one hundred and thirty pounds a week. One hundred and thirty pounds a week just to ride a motor-cycle – what a job!

'What do you do then?'

'I deliver things.'

Just then, a loud crackling voice started speaking from a speaker that was attached to a black plastic box at the rear of the cycle. 'Chopper!' the voice wailed. 'Where you been? I got clients on the phone an' dey screamin' at me. Wha'appen? Talk to me, boy.'

So this skinhead called Chopper did; talking into a small microphone, a little black thing, that hung from the handlebars. The voice wailed again, screaming and ranting some things about the importance of his client, and other things about his health and perhaps no job for Chopper if he didn't 'get his arse in gear'. He was plenty mad, this voice. Chopper put a glove in the speaker and when that did little to shut the voice up, he turned the radio off. When I asked him who it was that was screaming like that, Chopper sighed, saying it was Stanley. Stanley was the controller, the man that gave out the jobs, the man that made you money.

''ere,' said Chopper, 'take one of these.'

I took the sticker that he passed me and put it in my pocket. It was a Rocket Despatch sticker.

'Tell me,' I asked Chopper. 'How fast does that machine of yours go?'

He said some figure that I didn't believe possible and I watched him flick up the side-stand, start the motor, snick it into gear and drop the clutch. That machine made a hell of a racket, but it went really quick and I think he was showing off for my benefit – or maybe he was insulted that I did not look like I believed him. Whatever it was, he popped an enormous wheelie into the traffic after we said 'so long', and it made me smile.

Afterwards, I went down to the Arcade and got in a couple of games on the Invader machine before the money went dry. I was mighty pleased with myself for having topped the score, and left my autograph in the number one and two place on the electrical scoreboard thing. Then, with the sun out, I thought I'd go up to the park and see the ducks and get some kip on the grass. I saw a couple of jobs posted in these pretty grimy shop windows and I must say I wasn't tempted at all. It being only Wednesday and not the weekend, there weren't an awful lot of people in the park, except at lunch-time of course, when all the little secretaries came flooding into the place looking for a suntan. I didn't see many pretty ones though.

In the afternoon when the wind died it was quite hot. I fed the ducks with some of my choc-ice, I rode around and I slept under a big old oak. Come the evening, I was ravenous and even the sight of dear old mumma's cooking could not prevent me from putting fork to mouth. Jobtalk wasn't too bad though there was some mention of the possibility of a job at the Stock Exchange. For most of the dinner I was still in the dog-house over the matter of school – it normally took them about a week to adjust and so, after saying that I was sure I'd have more luck finding something in the morning and that I was feeling really tired having cycled all over the place today, I went to my room. Once inside, I locked the door and scarpered out the window onto our neighbour Mrs Brod's roof, clambered up the pipe to our roof and then once there I slipped down the fire stairs at the back and went to see my friend Jim.

Thursday I did pretty much the same as Wednesday. I played in the Arcade, walked in the park, I even went down the Kings Road to look at the freaks. Then, that night old Dad said he'd fixed everything up for me and I could start as a runner in this place in the City, on Monday.

Suits, just like school and what was worse, the hours were longer. And you were inside all day.

'No!' I cried.

'Yes, James. Monday.'

In desperation I said the first thing that came into my frightened mind. 'But I *have* a job!'

'You do? Well why didn't you tell us about it, James?' said my father. I could have sworn his face fell.

I was flailing now. 'I . . . I . . . ummh,' and then it came to me, as clear as water. 'I'm going to be a Despatch Rider! I found the job today. Went and had a little chat with the man that owns the place, but he's not completely sure I can start. But I'll find out tomorrow.'

'A *what?*' my mother said, and I told her and she asked me again and I explained it to her and then she said, 'Oh. How common.'

Thinking about it that night, it didn't seem such a bad idea. I'd be outside all day, it would certainly beat working in my dad's office, and besides I liked dirt bikes and had ridden a lot of them over the years. There was the small problem of having no machine to ride; but I soon overcame that, deciding to offer my services as a peddle man. And the more I started thinking about it the more enticing the idea became. I saw it as a Cowboys and Indians sort of thing. If you thought about it like that it could almost be fun. It was as if those men on the bikes were like the horse messengers in the West and everybody else – the cars, the cabs, the buses – were the savages. No better and no worse. Only if these savages ambush you by causing accidents, then scalping must be done to the wallet, before a rider can continue his perilous – no, adventurous – journey through the heartland of the metropolis.

I believe I slept with a smile on my face that night.

4

I called up Rocket Despatch next day, having left the house in the morning all smiles and 'I'll have a job this evening, you'll see's. Pedalling away up Sloane Street not knowing what I would say to these Rocket people but figuring that it was probably best if I called them up first to make an appointment or whatever it is you make when you go for a job. I tried about four boxes but each one of them was broken or smelt so bad from their dual role as toilet to the homeless that it was impossible to stay in the place without chucking up the breakfast. Finally I found this one box, off Lowndes Square, that was fit to dial from. I should have known to go to this place first because it was even richer than our area and the residents are all so frightened of being mugged, they make sure all the boxes work in case of mugging emergencies. I went in and put my 10p in the slot and dialled the number. Some West Indian man answered the phone and I told him I wanted to speak to the personnel department. He said I couldn't and I said why not and he said because he was out; so I asked him when he'd be back and I was looking up at the wall of this box, noticing that these places attract a lot of perverts that liked writing pervy things up on the wall. He said:

'Who wants to know?'

'I do.'

'Who are you?'

'My name is James.'

Then he made a stupid joke asking me if the name was James Bond and I told him that was a funny one, though I wished I hadn't because I didn't want to seem disrespectful. When he didn't answer I told him that my name was James Montgomery. Then he made this clicking sound, like a chicken farmer does when he's got to feed his chickens.

'D'you work for the tax man?' he said clicking again. I told him no.

'Ah, das all right den. 'ee be down the pub.'

Right then a little old lady wearing a coat that was too large and a hat with plastic fruit started making a rumpus on the window, rapping it with her knuckles. I ignored the impatient old bag and asked when the man would be back. Again the voice wanted to know, after a bit more chicken feeding, if I worked for the tax man.

'No,' I said. Then to the old bat who was starting to make faces at me and rapping with both hands, 'Go away.'

'What?' He said. She banged some more and I said, 'Go away.' 'Who?' he said, and I said not him but her and it took even longer to explain to him who she was and why I wanted her to go away and now she was getting out of hand and was trying to pull at the door of the box and I had to hold it closed until he told me that if I wanted a job I should come round after the pubs had shut. Then, he said, the personnel man would be there.

So I rolled up at this place off the Strand about five hours later. It was a right hole. The building was dilapidated and the brickwork was crumbling. I saw some motor-cycles parked outside with their radios squawking and a couple of riders lounging on them with their feet kicked up over the handlebars. Thinking that the best way to go into a place like this was to attract as little attention as possible, also feeling a little embarrassed about the lack of street muscle that I was riding, I parked my humble bicycle up the street – well, round the corner really.

The place was even worse on the inside. There were no

lights in the corridor, it had ripped-up lino and the only clue to the whereabouts of the offices was a small tattered cardboard sign and arrow pointing upwards through the crotch of a naked lady hanging above. It was really dark and then I started hearing this howling chant. I was sure it was Indian until I heard the word 'laxative' repeated three or four times. He was a hairy man, the man that was making this noise. I tried asking him where I could find Godfrey, the personnel man, but he was unable to tell me, I think he was deeply involved in some sort of ritualistic chant and this necessitated the constant hopping up and down and clasping of stomach. Seeing that the hairy was unable to help much I went on up another floor. I met another rider, none too friendly, who looked at me up and down when I asked him if he knew where Godfrey was. He wore this wax-cotton suit. Then the bastard laughed at me and then walked off. Naturally, my impressions of the place weren't so wonderful and I was all ready just to turn round and walk out but then I started thinking about the city job so I went on walking.

On the second floor I found two doors, both battered; on one was written 'Riders' and on the other 'Babylon'. There was music playing in Babylon, this loud cranky West Indian music, and I knocked which was stupid because there was no way anybody would hear and when nobody heard I walked in.

'What you want, boy?' asked this large and very black looking gentleman. He sat at an old desk behind a bank of telephones and on one side there was the music machine.

'Is this Rocket Despatch?' I said.

'It ain't church, boy.' said the comedian. There were a lot of naked ladies hanging on the wall.

'I've come to see Godfrey about a job,' said I; but before he had a chance to answer, every phone on the desk started ringing and flashing and demanding attention and this man set to, with an industry that my mother would have been proud of. The box was switched off, and he went into his patter, answering all these inquiries, scribbling all the time, smiling and smooth talking them all. When he was done, the box was turned back on and I asked him if he could help.

'You wanna' job?'

'Yes.'

'You gotta bike?'

'That's right, I've got a Raleigh.'

'Dat a vintage machine?' he said, scratching himself. I heard an awful lot of sniggering coming from the adjoining room and they would have sniggered an awful lot more if Stanley hadn't told them to shut it.

'It's ten years old,' I said.

'Is it a motor-cycle?'

'No. It's a push bike.'

'Boy,' he said. 'Why you waste my time?'

I shrugged and Stanley fed the chickens.

Then the chicken feeder pointed behind him to a large map of London and the Home Counties and told me that that was the area he worked because they were a 'dee-stance firm' with a lot of clients 'dat 'ad business in the countryside' and to conclude he asked me if I'd ever been to the country on that push-bike of mine and I said quite rightly, 'I've been to Milton Keynes.'

'How long did it take you?'

'Two days.'

This the chicken feeder thought magnificently funny and nearly socked a hole in his desk with all that glee he was pounding out. Then he threw his neck up to howl like wolves do; then he scratched himself. Finally he managed to get out a sentence without choking himself. He said:

'Some of my riders can make it dere an' back in under ninety minutes providing, of course, dere be no complication wid' de law.'

Well that was that I thought. I'd tried and I'd made an

idiot of myself. What I did then was to just make sure there was no work for a peddle man like meself.

'No,' said Stanley. 'But who it was dat told you?'

'I did,' said a voice from nearby. And when I turned I saw the car beater Chopper. He had a bandage around one of his big boots.

'Well, well,' said Chopper. 'The idle rich no longer rich enough? Come about a job, 'ave you?'

'That's right,' said I.

'So why you tell him, Chopper? You 'aven't the most friendly of nature at de best of times.'

What happened next was that Chopper explained to the man whom he called Stanley, how it was that he knew me 'like', and how it was, 'like', that I had acted as witness, 'like', and then he went on to say how he'd broken his 'bleedin' toe' when he kicked the car and that he found it terribly difficult to walk; how they made 'A' reg Mini's of much stronger metal than the old 'P's and Q's' that buckled easily under a hefty boot. He swore about the car, the driver and his toe, and then at Stanley for trying to interrupt him in the middle of his gripe. Then they talked about how Chopper needed a 'friggin' pillion' if he was to continue working and then I said I would be 'absolutely perfect' for the job and they frowned at the use of the word 'absolutely' but sort of half agreed that I might be all right; but under no circumstances was I to expect to be paid much – they both agreed on that – though they argued over how much was to be deducted from Chopper's pay for my pay. And in the end I had a job on a one week's trial, starting Monday.

5

So that was how I came to have gainful employment and when I left that office, I felt pretty pleased with myself. But that feeling was a little peculiar because I was never a one to think that I would have to work so early and it was even more peculiar when I got home that night to eat dinner with the fossils. Old mumma dear – her face when I told her; I could have shot a whole role of Polaroid film, easily. It had everything in it – all those facial movements from happiness (when I told her I had a job) to complete amazement, to dreadful shock. It must be said, though, that her face in shock doesn't make much of a picture with all that skin that droops down under her chin. Father voiced his approval in between lengthy chewing sessions and little Pook contributed, not in the best way, by saying this:

'You going to be a despatch rider, James' (now he made a hearty laugh) 'but you haven't got a bike and Oh! You know the garden opposite Ecclestone Square?' And I said I did. 'Well, we were all going over there to play football in the lunch-break and just as we were about to cross, me and Holbrook' (mother corrected him here, saying Holbrook and I) 'saw this despatch rider bloke come tearing down the street like this' (he lifted up his paw, started making howling noises and I watched as the paw shot across the table just missing the pepper pot) '. . . until he got near us, *then* this stupid doggie steps off the curb into the road. And what do you think happens?'

Mother said: 'I don't think we want to hear about it at the table dea . . .'

'*Boom*!' said Pook and simultaneously crashed his two paws together over the crushed potatoes, and smiled.

Well, that sort of thing was just what she needed to sink her jaws into, and in no time at all she was firing away on all cylinders. I heard every cliché in the book as she tried to dissuade me from joining up on the bikes and instead to join up in the city. Even Dad couldn't take it and got up from his seat saying he was awfully tired, that work today had been a nightmare, and that he had a small toothache (I had already warned him about the potatoes). And for him, getting away from the table was fairly easy – not like for us, the offspring. We almost have to beg to get down unless every scrap on the plate is finished. Hence the reason for our being so adamant that the dog, Jack, should be allowed into the dining room at dinner-time. Sometimes, even the dog wouldn't eat the food we slipped to him under the tablecloth.

So I listened to her and smiled, thinking that was the best tactic and knowing perfectly well that no matter what you say to her, she's not going to listen anyway so there's no point in saying it. Ten minutes passed and old mumma was on her way to a new nagging record and both me and Pook had a couple of potatoes left and some of her stew and the going wasn't easy. Pook made a couple of passes at the dog but he wouldn't have any of it, then I slipped him a potato cunningly disguised in a coat of ketchup and Pook called me a cheat. I sacrificed my stomach for my ears and finished my plate. Now mumma was just winding up and then the little brat got her going again (to pay me back for having unloaded some food on the dog) this time by saying how unfair it was that he had to do homework and how he was thinking of getting himself thrown out because he hated it so much. Give a dog a bone and watch it gnaw.

'See what kind of example you set for your younger brother? Can you hear what he's saying? Can you?'

Of course, Pook loved this and I saw him sniggering away behind his napkin as old mother got into the swing of things. Luckily for me she was also her biggest fan when it came to cooking, and when I knew that dad was asleep in front of the TV I waited for her to reach for thirds and then legged it out the room. She yelled at me as I went but once in the safety of my room, I had that door locked, the stereo headphones wrapped around the ears, and things were peaceful once again.

The next couple of days passed without much happening, with the weekend being right there, the fossils were out socialising and I had the house pretty much to myself and when they did come in, I soon went to ground. And before I knew it, Monday was on me.

I woke up early, being excited and sort of nervous about things, and when I looked out the window, it was grey and overcast with a hint of some storm clouds towards the Thames area. I made breakfast whilst the house was still asleep, eating cereal and eggs and bacon, and then dressed up in many layers. I slipped out the house after saying goodbye to Pook, thinking I may never see him again – this being such a perilous/adventurous job – and made my way up to Bowater House. Well, Chopper's the sort of person that I never thought could be any place on time; but he was that day, and at a quarter to nine he was there over the other side of the road yelling.

'*Oi!*' he shouted as he was never one for names. I went over, crossing through the traffic, and he undid the strap that fastened a helmet to the back of the machine and passed it to me. I said:

'Morning,' and, 'Do you think it'll rain?'

He wasn't too sure. With the visor of the helmet up, he then told me how I should behave sitting on the rear of such a machine. He said:

'It ain't difficult, just remember to lean when I lean. Don't sit upright when I've got her laid over in a corner, like, 'coz if you do, it don't do me no good whatsoever and you might find your Lordship flying frew the air in a most unlordly manner only to wipe your botty on that nasty rough black looking stuff they call the road. Understand?'

I told him I did and probably started shaking. He went on:

'Also, behind me, 'ere,' and Chopper pointed to this rail thing on the rear of the cycle, 'is what's called a grab-rail. This you 'old wiv yer two hands to stop unnecessary movement on the seat and stop me from fumping you if you move too much, got it?'

'Yes. How's your foot?'

'Magnificent, thank you.'

He was a sarcky bugger all right, that Chopper; but things got better with him once you knew him. Right then, though, I thought he was a rotten piece of work.

The gears ground metal on metal, sounding as first was engaged, and when the light went green we shot off, me holding on with the devil, rolling across three lanes to make an illegal U-turn to go down the Cromwell Road. I was a little worried at first that we were going to go too fast, but seeing the long lines of traffic stretching way down past Harrods, I settled on my perch to enjoy the view. There were shoppers and others going to work everywhere. And the bastard didn't slow – we ended up running down the lanes in between the lanes. We must have been going twenty to thirty miles an hour faster than the cars. I thought maybe old Chopper was putting on a show for my benefit, playing up sort of thing, but after a bit I soon realised that this was the way the man rode. He was mightily skilful as a motor-cycle pilot and we swooped all over the road looking for the quickest line through the snarled mess of cars.

I was sitting on the back, all goggle eyed, holding on white-knuckle-tight to the grab-rail and making properly sure that the old knees were tucked in tight, so as not to get them chopped off. It didn't take much time to reach North End Road where we stopped at the light and I asked where we were going. Old Chopper said that the airport was the place we were going, only most of what he said was lost as he opened up the motor to go for the green and leave all the cars in our wake. That machine had some acceleration. The motor was good sounding, too. Like a rumbling and a bubbling sound deep down in the polished steel pipe and sometimes, in between shifts, you could hear the whoosh of air as the carbs sucked it down. Then he started to wind it on. On the white broken line, in the centre of the big flyover at Hammersmith, we ran at seventy-five, eighty. This was between the cars already on the road. Then, you could feel the vibration coming up through the footpegs and, with the visor open, tears started streaming down my face. At the next light, we stopped and Chopper said:

'You like it?'

It was fine, this riding, and I told him so. We went then, when the light went green, going into a roundabout and being dropped over so near the road that I could have reached out with my arm and touched it. And then Chopper brought the machine upright and rolled it over the other way, to make the left off the roundabout and onto the dual carriageway, pulling like a train up through the gears with me leaning forward as much as possible. Soon we were running in top with four thousand on the clock, doing ninety and the old adrenalin was pumping away better than any cog and gear system in any motor.

We ran up onto the flyover and I saw just the other side of a hundred when he had to shut her down for a couple of cars meandering lazily through the turn ahead. The Hillman driver didn't have a clue about much and being a little old and fuzzy in the head, refused to move. So we took him on the inside giving him a one-finger salute on the way.

Now we were running on the open road rushing down the shallow incline where the two black lanes fan out to make three brown ones, and the wind was blowing strong and hard, and my head wanted to rest, and that big red speedo needle was hovering somewhere around the one twenty mark, and the motor and wind noise was enormous. Here is where he shut her down, and I was damned if I could see anything ahead that might cause him to do that. No cars ahead, just open road. We rode around a bend up ahead and, sitting pretty up on a ramp, just to the side of the layby were the police. We were doing sixty-nine miles an hour and Chopper was laughing.

At the airport, I had to run in with this envelope to a little lady sitting at the British Airways desk, get her signature and that was it. The job was done. Chopper called in on the radio to Stanley but because of the buildings and the range we couldn't hear a single word he said. So we rode out and parked up on the layby on the interlink road that connected the airport with the M4. Then we climbed the grass bank about halfway and there we sat in the morning sun that had only just started to poke through the grey. I watched the cars and Chopper had a good smoke. I had plenty of things whirling through the brain. I saw that whole route – from Bowater House to the grass bank. I had it memorised; it had to be the best ride I'd ever had and that includes some of those fancy rides in the Amusement parks, and even the water slides. I saw it all. But Chopper was pretty restless and kept stamping his heels into the earth, grinding at it and then doing it some more. Eventually, he said:

'You got a girl?'

'Nope.'

'I thought you rich bastards had tons of birds. I'm always reading about it in the bleedin' papers. How you all go off to these friggin' parties, get plastered and then get your nickers off. Every bleedin' day I read about it.'

'Well I'd certainly like to join in, certainly I would. I never go to parties like that.'

'You don't?'

'Nope.'

'So why ain't you got a bird?'

'I don't know. I haven't met one.'

This was the truth. Every school I got sent to: always boys, never any sweet little ladies. So then Chopper asks me if I was one of them and I said, 'One of whom?' and he said, 'You know, one of *those*.' And things weren't much clearer to me until he sort of dropped his wrist and pouted. Then I laughed and he laughed too and I said, 'Poufter?'

'Yeah.'

'No.'

'Thank the fucking Lord. I had some 'orrible notion that I was stuck, like, with some flaming faggot that would do the nasties to me. It's just like my luck, the way it's running at the moment.'

So then we talked about his luck and he told me about his sweetheart, a lady skinhead called Sherry and how he ''ad sneakin' suspicions that she was doin' a nasty' on him. He told me that a nasty in this instance was when she was seeing another skin. He knew this because she polished her Doctor Martens and in the past she had never done such things. So I said that perhaps she was taking an interest in her appearance and he said 'Good one!' and asked if I had been eating fish for breakfast on account of my spectacular brain activity.

Old Chopper – he could make a boy feel a fool through such sarckiness. I sort of shut up there and perhaps even sulked a bit. Up above, a 747 came in screaming and I watched it descend right down until it was hidden by some buildings and the cars kept streaming past. I got out some old chewing gum that I had found hidden in my Barbour and when I peeled a piece, doing it right out in the open,

Chopper wanted some and as it was the last stick, I had to break it in two.

Still being quiet, he said 'Ta,' and then went on to tell me about himself and the problems of going out with a Spurs supporter if you're West Ham and that, at the local derbys, they had to make an agreement, a mutual one, to only watch the match on the telly, in case the two of them came into contact in the crowd violence that always went on before and after the game, in which case, 'like', they'd both be worried sick about the other and wouldn't be able to fight 'proper like'. 'You know, we wouldn't be able to enjoy it.'

'Right.' I said.

'I mean,' Chopper said, 'what's the point in going to a football match if you can't have a bloody good ruck?'

'The football?'

'Nah. If you just want to watch the football, you stay at 'ome where it's nice an' warm with the telly an' the wife an' the tea. Nah, you don't go to a football match just for the the football, I mean, don't be stupid your Lordship.'

'I'm not a Lord.'

'Well you've got money incha?'

'That doesn't mean I'm a Lord.'

'All right, squire, I wos only kiddin',' he said. 'Nah, you see you go to football to let out your tension after a nasty week, like don'cha'? I mean, it stands to bloody reason, dunnit?'

It didn't; but Chopper thought it made plenty fine sense and expounded on his theory, saying that the government was entirely to blame, of course; that if there weren't such rotten unemployment people might be a 'lit'l betah behaved' and that apart from all of those reasons – it was a good laugh anyway. Then he asked if I liked football and I had to tell him that I hadn't been and he said that he'd take me because he thought I was 'all right'.

Right then I liked Chopper – he was mighty different

from the rest and no doubt about it, he was a rogue, but an affable and likeable one and I was thinking then that maybe we were going to have some fun. In a little while, Stanley started squawking on the radio, 'Two one, two one!' and old Chopper went limping down the hill and after he had talked to him we were given another job and he beckoned to me to come down. Soon we were riding again on the M4 with the sun on our backs and the wind blowing.

It was a pick-up from a copy bureau, a regular run, to an old codger that ran some aircraft magazine from his home some twenty-five miles away in a small village to the north and east of Slough. Once we had dumped it and called Stanley and found out that there was nothing to be had up in our neck of the woods, we headed back into town on a road that cut back and forth across the faces of small green hills where sheep grazed and here the air was fresh and good smelling. The road went this way for a few miles. When we came to a humpback he gunned the cycle and played with the bridge, using it to toss the front wheel right up – so it was almost vertical, just like we did on dirt bikes. We rode along a narrow country lane and this road took us, leisurely, past farms and tractors and barns and long steel mesh fences. It felt good sitting up there and when I looked back the smoke from the exhausts made a curtain across the lane. Soon we were back on a dual carriageway heading south, doing eighty.

I was looking up at the old clouds and now the blue sky, thinking how agreeable this sort of work could be, when this machine came blitzing by on the inside. So fast he came by, and close too. Nearly made me fall off with the shock as I wasn't expecting nobody to come by us cruising at the speed we were going. This man opened up a lot of road between us in no time at all. Chopper hated him for it. He probably took it as an insult, like a slap in the face, for another despatch rider to pass him with such disrespect; and in no time at all, Chopper had that 860 Honda we were riding pegged at the red line.

Up ahead all the cars started moving out the way – I guess the other rider flashed them way in advance.

Now, I was worried. I had my chin perched on the shoulder of Chopper, and I had my eyes half-open as I was too scared to keep them shut and I was trying terribly hard not to think about the consequences of an accident. About what would happen if one of the long line of seemingly slow-moving cars should pull out, or if we should hit a rock, or have a flat, or . . . – and there were just too many 'or's. So I had a little talk with God to see if he could sort of help me out here. It had been an awful long time since we had talked and I felt a little rusty, and not being a Catholic, I had to wait a while. In the end I wasn't entirely sure we had even talked but I felt a little better. Edified is the word I think you use here.

With my eyes wide open I saw that the road ran down a small hill to a roundabout and that the other messenger on his twin exhaust-bulk-of-a-machine had started to slow down when he came to the stripes on the road. This is where we brake, I was thinking, smiling. The stripes came and we blitzed onto them. *This* is where we brake, I was thinking, half-smiling. The three chevron distance board came and went. If we brake now it is too late anyway I was thinking as we shot past the troublemaker and *then*, we went on the brakes. The whole machine shook violently, the rear end squealed as he locked it up and I shut my eyes and did some quiet squealing too.

I waited to be thrown but instead I was pitched into a corner. Like the machine had been dropped on its left side. The metal of Chopper's rear-set footpeg ground into the tarmac and sparked as we went down a couple of gears. We had a couple of lengths on him as Chopper flipped the bike over the other way, up and straight over and down so we cornered at the same angle with the footpeg grounding, sparking. Now we were going round to the right, carving a line between two cars before we went up and over again to take the London turning. Here, he tried it, coming up on the outside by the aarmco; but old Chopper just ran wide, shutting the door on him.

Third, fourth, fifth, sixth we went and then flat out with the road straight and empty and hilly and the wind howling and the bike shaking over some ripples on the road. The crest of a hill, where the sky met it, and at the bottom two trucks side by side filling the lanes.

He tried it again; but again the door was shut as we took to the white line – the only line through. He was mad with us and bawled on his horn. We kept on, and into the rolling corridor we went; into and out of and then buffeted by disturbed air tumbling off the cabs. I turned as we came out but he didn't come – all that rubber and steel worried him.

We lost him at the traffic light a little further on when we ran the red. When I opened my eyes Chopper was slapping his thighs and haw-hawing.

6

We stopped at an Esso station on the North Circular and the bike was being filled with four star and I had been to the toilet and vomited, twice.

'You'll get used to it.' Chopper said.

'I hope so.'

I sat outside, up against a brick wall and my hands shook and my belly was awful and I cursed everybody I could think of starting with the headmaster, working my way through certain members of my family, and ending with the other despatch rider. Afterwards, we did a couple of small jobs – a W1, W2 and a WC2.

At lunchtime we rode back to the Strand and parked the bike outside Rocket.

Motor-cycles were parked everywhere: on the pavement standing on their side-stands; standing in the road perpendicular to the curb; leaning up against lamp-posts; and some rested against the wall of the small funeral service business opposite. All the radios were squawking.

Vera's was a small cafeteria with a glass front, large red letters, and was just one door down from Rocket. We walked in and went up to the counter.

''allochopperluvall right?' this large lady with curlers in her hair asked.

'Not bad, Vera. Thank you.'

'Good,' said Vera, buttering a whole loaf, one slice after the other in rapid succession.

Then she asked who I was and Chopper not being the best of name rememberers, didn't remember. So I told her and we shook hands. She had calloused hands. Then we ordered. Chopper had food and I had only tea for the belly was still queasy. Afterwards we went and sat at one of the tables and Chopper started smoking. I had a look about and the whole place was full of these leather-clothed riders shuffling in and out with their lunch or their coffee in suits that were old and worn and tattered. I put down my helmet.

'Frankie,' said Chopper. 'All right?'

When I looked up Frankie was standing at the end of our table, staring and saying nothing. There was something strange about him right then, something peculiar, as if the man was looking at us and seeing us but not seeing anything at all. That is how Frankie is. Added to which he was wearing the uniform of a mounted policeman.

'Frank, this is er . . . um . . .'

I told him my name and made a pleased-to-meet-you sort of smile half expecting a response, but Frank didn't respond and instead sat at the table, pulling out from his pocket as he did so a small clockwork policeman. He wound him up, put him on the table and let him go.

'Frankie,' said Chopper. 'I've told you once if I've told you a faarsand times, *don't bring the little bugger in 'ere.* I don't like him. He gives me the jitters.'

Frankie, the man with the faraway eyes, did not, I think, hear any of the things said by Chopper, and he put a pepper pot in the path of the walking policeman. Before the policeman had a chance to make an arrest, Chopper whisked him away.

Frank's eyes bulged. He started humming. The tune, I think was 'The Professionals'.

'Bodie, Doyle,' said Frank. 'Take the rear. You lot,' he said to a group of tourists who had sat at the table opposite, 'Come with me.' All of this was said with a Scottish accent and once he'd said it he darted under the table.

Me, I realised that this man wasn't altogether normal,

so I got up and pretended that tea was what I wanted and wandered over to order one.

'Now you just be'ave,' Chopper barked. 'Last time, remember wot 'appened last time. I ain't goin' to get banned again so *cut it out!*'

Frankie came up for air, banging his head as he did so and sending Chopper's tea spilling copiously into his lap. As he scurried out of the way Chopper said, in a voice that could have woken the dead:

'Nah look wot you fuckin' done you fuckin' bastard.'

'Ah, so sorry old chap,' said Frankie. 'Watson, bring the man a cloth.'

Old Vera picked up a cloth, slung it and Frank caught it.

'Now, you wanna trade, huh? Hand over the kid and nobody gets hurt. Understand, punk?' This Frank said like Humphrey Bogart and he held out his hands; one was open and in the other he held the cloth. They traded and once Noddy was returned safely, old Frankie cooed gently in the little doll's ear, 'It's swell to have you back, kid, just swell.'

Then dinner came and the two of them behaved, settling down to eat all the eggs and beans and sausages and chips and bacon and tomatoes that were heaped in a steaming pile on their plates. And oh did I suddenly have a terrible appetite seeing the lady, a beautiful one, that brought the food to the table. She was maybe five six with white hair that was cut short and square, with lips that sort of pouted and were red, and big blue eyes and little ears with large gold circular earrings. So I quickly ordered some food and Chopper smiled and said something about him thinking that I did not have an appetite and it being curious that I should find one, 'all of a sudden, like' and of course I denied that there was any link between my appetite and the lady that brought the food to the table.

When the food came I ate heartily, having completely forgotten the queasiness in my belly and the ride in the morning. When I finished, the girl, whose name I learned was Kath, came to the table and took my plate away asking me if I wanted anything else. God, I liked her. 'I'll have some more tea,' I said all dreamy. And she brought this and asked again and I said biscuits and again and I said cake. And Chocolate bars. And Danish patries. And fruit and finally when the belly was big and bloated, the bill. Kath smiled (such a sweet, pouting and warm smile) and told me that I'd have to pay Vera. I was sick, both in the belly and in the heart.

When we had paid (me trying terribly hard not to appear too interested) Chopper asked me if my mother fed me. I had to tell him that she was not a wonderful cook but he didn't look like he believed me.

Outside we walked along the street and in the road motor-cycles were coming and leaving, some going fast. The wind was blowing and polystyrene cups used by the riders, now empty, broken and dirty, flew up in the gusts and one whipped along under the wind's power until the wind stopped and it fell motionless in the gutter, by me. Away to the north, a couple of buildings over, you could hear the traffic from the Strand moving along and I was thinking. The thing was this: how it was when I was a toddler out for walks with my mother, and how, having size and age on his side, a toddler could get away with just about anything; and if skirts should take his fancy, big billowing beautiful ones, then a toddler could toddle up to skirts and sort of pull them and laugh and the skirt owner would laugh thinking that it was so funny that the toddler found it so funny and the only one that didn't find it so funny was mother who simply found it embarrassing and tiresome. Mother was the one that would have to rush over to rescue the lady, disengage the sweaty, grubby fingers of the little laughing brute, apologise profusely and lead me off whilst I was still laughing like a champion. And this happened on many occasions and I only remembered it

44

because the skirt the girl with the white hair wore was similar to a skirt worn by a lady that used to sunbathe in the garden opposite the flat.

So we walked in the street past Hondas and worn Suzukis and large Kawasakis and two-stroke Yamahas, and Chopper pointed out which machines belonged to whom and when we came to a white Police 650 BMW, Chopper said the machine belonged to Frank. I saw written on the panniers the word 'Polite'. Next to it there was a machine with long trailed forks, a chromed teardrop tank and swept back handlebars. This machine was Rita's and it was chromed metal, a lot of it, and black and shiny.

'Who's Rita?' I asked and Chopper pointed down an alley where two people stood in the shadows, talking.

'The one wiv the long 'air. She owns the heap,' he said and then he shouted: 'Rita!'

When Rita came out she was tucking things in all her pockets and the other long hair walked off down the street. This Rita was tall and sort of big boned, well, fat is a better description but we shall leave it as big boned. She had black hair, long and and none too clean. On her back she had a leather jerkin embroidered with ornament chains and a picture of a red tiger, roaring. Underneath, in bold white block lettering were the words 'HELL'S ANGELS, ENGLAND'. I saw this in the reflection of the car window that she stood in front of. Her mascara was thick and heavier than my mum's. We stood in front of each other as she looked me up and then down.

'Who's this then?' she asked.

'Umm . . .' said Chopper. And then, suddenly, it came to him. *'John!'*

'No, James,' said I.

'A mind the size of a pea,' said Rita.

'He told me John, didn't ya?'

'No, James.'

'You didn't hear me. I'll say it again and I'll say it

slowly this time. *You . . .told . . . me . . .your . . .name . . . was . . . John*, didn't you?'

He was sort of half snarling when he said this and those knuckles of his were doing the crab-walk.

'Right, John. No doubt about it, must have been thinking of someone else when I said – '

'But you can call 'im James,' said Chopper.

Then it was explained what I was doing and how I was helping the invalid Chopper. As Rita had not heard the story of Chopper's foot, that was told also.

After, they talked motor-cycle talk and Chopper was all excited about this machine, the new FJ1100 and quoted all sorts of performance figures at her but she was none too impressed and said that that type of machine wasn't motor-cycling and he said well what is it then and Rita was stumped and wasn't too sure but was sure that it wasn't motor-cycling. Then they argued about what motor-cycling is and from what I understood Rita seemed to think that getting dirty (doing motor-cycle maintenance) was an integral and highly important part of the motor-cycle experience. Chopper scoffed at this and Rita got insulted and threatened to 'club' him if he didn't watch his lip. Here, Chopper made a joke pushing out his lip to look at it and none of us thought much of this joke, So now, a little bit sulky, Chopper said we had to go and 'earn our crust' and we left.

In the afternoon we tottered around the city and I ran up and down the stairs making drops in employment bureaus and up and down the elevators for the banking companies and the insurance companies.

Come six o'clock I was tired and all ready to go home and we'd just done a drop to Apex Travel Ltd, when Stanley gave us an option (if ya dohn't take it, ya not be workin' much tomorra, said he) on a job picking up in the City and dropping in Coulsdon, the other side of Croydon. We took it, running out with the rush-hour traffic, picking up petrol in Balham on the way and we didn't get back to London before a quarter to eight and I didn't get home before quarter past, seventy-five minutes late.

7

She was ready and waiting and had adopted a strategic position behind her bedroom door. I should have known that the coast was not clear the moment I opened the door and was not immediately greeted with audible sounds of a dinner in progress. Then, I should have retreated to the rear of the building, gone up to the roof, and then descended the drainpipe commando style and entered the flat via my bedroom window.

Instead, I was caught in a terrible cross-fire. My father appeared from the lounge and my mother from her bedroom. As soon as the pair of them appeared in the hallway the dog leapt up from his resting place by the radiator and disappeared down the corridor, yelping.

'Where have you been?' they said simultaneously. 'Why are you late? What have you been doing? Who have you been doing it with? Dinner was an hour ago,' etc., etc.

I had to do an enormous amount of grovelling and lying and blame-shifting before I was allowed through to the kitchen, to fish out the incinerated remains of the remains of dinner (Mother having forgotten to turn the oven to a lower number).

'Delicious!' I said, in an attempt to stem the barrage of verbal abuse that had followed me down the corridor, and into the kitchen.

'. . . and another thing, James. I'm not running a hotel here. When I set a time for dinner, I expect *you* to have the courtesy to turn up on time. I'm not the hired help around here, you know!'

This was certainly true; the hired help was younger, prettier and certainly more tolerant. Just then, the doorbell went. Two minutes later, Pook came running past the kitchen.

'It's her,' he screamed, 'it's Juicy. Take cover!'

He disappeared down the corridor and the dog disappeared with him.

'Hallowooo!' shrieked a high and piercing voice from along the corridor. It was high and piercing to start with and by the time it had travelled down the snaking corridor it was hideously distorted into a frightful wail, a banshee-like scream.

'We're in here, darling,' my mother shrieked in return.

There were ominous sounds coming from the floorboards and soon there was an ominous shape.

Miss Lucy, my mother's dearest friend, was almost as tall as she was wide and had a knack of making even the most expensive and well-coutured clothes look like rags picked fresh from a dustcart. They were oiled, soiled, badly creased and crumpled.

She waddled up to the table, floorboards lamenting her arrival, and seeing me struggling with my food, said:

'Darling, what a surprise! You're home early. What's the matter with you? Are you sick? Has he got a temperature?'

From the corner of my eye I could see old Mother making strange gestures with her hands, pit signals. Lucy, not known as a lady well endowed with grey matter, in fact not known as anything other than well endowed, knotted her brow, obviously puzzled. Then she thought Mother was playing some sort of game and started imitating her.

'Is he sick?' she asked, doing the hand-jive.

'Not physically,' said my mother.

'Oh, well, school isn't over yet, is it?'

'No, not yet.'

'Oh, I see. You've been, um . . .'

'Expelled,' I said, not wishing to embarrass her.

'Oh dear, darling. How tiresome!' she said. 'You must have been a naughty boy. What did you do this time? Sorry, sorry, I shouldn't have asked that. How awful of me!'

'That's all right,' I said, 'I don't mind . . .'

'I know *you* don't mind. It's your mother I'm thinking about. Poor darling, it must be absolutely frightful for you. Are you bearing up all right?'

Mother was quick off the mark with that one; seizing the opportunity for a good wallow, she exclaimed:

'I think so. But life, isn't it so *cruel*!'

Taking a last look at Lucy, dressed this evening in a Cossack's uniform with boots and pantaloons matching in colour but not in style, I slowly edged my way out of the kitchen hoping to take refuge behind the closed doors of my bedroom as they talked about some old codger, impotent and limp, that Lucy had found by the bar at some rich club the night before.

I was half-way down the hall when she called. I explained that I was in the middle of battle stations, having to evacuate my bowels before they evacuated my senses. She granted me leave and I left, turning right into the bathroom and shutting and locking the door. When the storm had passed I went to my room to rest on my bed. I could hear their voices drift down the corridor, punctuated every now and then by the short staccato squeal of old Lucy exercising her lungs.

Something moved underneath the bed. I felt it move. It made a sound and I heard it. Then two heads popped out from underneath; one was smiling and the other was grinning. It was Pook and Jack, Jack being our Jack Russell terrier.

'What are you doing in here?' I asked.

'Lucy. Oh my God . . . She made a grab for me at the

front door. I ducked and ran off and she threatened to come after me . . .'

He stopped in mid-sentence. His face was ashen, almost white. Footsteps were coming down the hall. There were giants on the loose.

'You think it's . . . Lucy?' Pook muttered nervously. I joined him under the bed and the three of us waited, and watched, and listened.

We heard her open and close the door of the spare room. We couldn't see her because the bedroom door obstructed the view but we could hear her. The whole building could hear her.

'Pooohoook!' she wailed in a voice that started about three octaves away from where it finished. And it finished two octaves above middle C which meant that the place where it started was a place most ears couldn't go without breaking. We covered our ears.

Now was the time for quick thinking; but quick thinking was not easy when terror and cold fear gripped every bone in your body; all asphyxiating and completely debilitating. Like suffering from the effects of having a plastic bag wrapped and secured around the old head.

'What shall we do?' I said.

'The dog,' Pook replied. 'Watch.'

He lifted Jack's ears and started saying, over and over, the word 'Kill'. This had the effect of making the dog, normally very placid, bare its teeth and growl. Lucy was not far away. Opening the door, she uttered our names but was greeted only with the sight of a small hound rushing out from underneath the bedspread, barking. Before she had a chance to retreat, old Jack, our faithful and trust-worthy hound, attached himself firmly to the heel of her boot. Lucy yelped. When she stopped yelping, she started screaming and when she stopped screaming she tried walking. None of this had any effect on the dog. He thought it was all a good game and was thoroughly enjoying himself. We laughed until we cried. Then Mother came in and spoiled it all by swiping the little pooch across the rump. He squealed and fled back to us under the bed.

'Oh God, what has he done to your boots?' my mother asked, looking down at the puntured boot. We shuffled back, just out of sight.

'It's nothing, nothing at all.' said Lucy, lying.

I could see the hole from under the bed and it was a beaut.

'Whatever could have got into the brute,' Lucy said. 'He was quite rabid. Has he gone bonkers or something?'

'I don't know,' Mother said. 'He's never behaved that way before. Where'd he go?'

I glanced at Pook. He was having great difficulty suppressing his laughter.

'He went under there!' said Lucy with as much disdain as she could muster, which wasn't much.

We shuffled back as far as we could and waited to be discovered. It didn't take long.

'James! Pook! What in God's name are you two doing down there? Come out right this instant!'

We came out; but slowly. Jack stayed behind – he was no fool. We sat on the bed and smiled, the two of us, hoping to placate her inevitable outburst. We would have had more success pissing against a force ten.

'Who did it?' she barked.

'The dog,' I said, regretting having said it almost instantaneously. She gave me a verbal lashing for that and then went on with more complicated questions, like who was responsible. I was stumped for an answer but not Pook. Never Pook. He always has an answer for everything, even the weather.

'It was the fur on her boots, Mum,' he said smiling up at her. She took a deep and troubled breath.

'What do you mean "the fur on her boots"?'

'That fur,' said Pook, pointing at the orange fur rim. 'It looks like Tabby fur and Jack here . . .'

Lucy cut him off.

'It's jolly well not cat fur,' said old Lucy, a little outraged. 'I paid a bloody fortune for these boots and I take that as an insult. Apologise!'

Pook burped. Then he said:

'I'm sorry, Lucy; but if you'd just let me finish what I was saying, I'd say that the dog probably thought that you were wearing a cat on your boots. And he hates cats, he really does, honest.'

I chipped in: 'It's the truth Lucy. You have got to believe him.'

'Are you saying that the reason the dog attacked *me* was because *he* thought my boots were a pair of cats?'

'Yes, that's about it,' we said.

Well it wasn't about it. Mother didn't believe a word of what he had said and said so. We were told to apologise. After, Pook was sent to his room escorted by Juicy. I was left alone, unarmed and helpless with my angry mother. Then there was a few minutes of deathly silence and much fidgeting before she started and when she did there was a small scream from down the hall followed by a terrible female laughing sound. Poor Pook, I thought. Poor, poor Pook.

Mother was in full flight. 'You treat this house like a cheap hotel, James. You have absolutely no respect for me or your father or the family unit, have you?'

I did not answer. I had found over the years that the best way of dealing with her lectures was to keep quiet and think of other things Marie for example or Kath. Sweet, sweet Kath.

'Are you listening to me, James? James!'

'I'm listening, Mother.'

'Well, what in God's name is wrong with you? Why you late for supper? Why do you persistently get thrown out of schools? Why aren't you like all the other nice boys from your school? What's wrong with you? Are you angry? Are you? Is there chip on your shoulder or something, James? If so, why? Why, James, why?'

This was all news to me. I hadn't a clue what she was talking about and told her so. She said it all over again for my benefit, and at the end of the second explanation I still hadn't a clue. At the end of the third explanation I pleaded fatigue. Unfortunately this did not stop her and she carried on threatening me until I fell asleep. And then she left. Life seemed so much simpler on the back of a motorcycle.

8

I liked it. I realised that, that evening when I lay in bed unable to sleep. I tried thinking of sheep; but for each sheep that I thought of, the beast would transmogrify. The hair, all white, soft, and fluffy would darken perceptibly; the horns would form a black, shiny membrane that wrapped around the skull, secured by a band, and the form of propulsion changed from four legs to two wheels. Then the bugger would disappear out of frame leaving a cloud of smoke and a pile of droppings.

I tried thinking of Kath but that was also unsuccessful.

Each time she came to the table to take an order, the sheep starting bleating outside the back door and she hurried off, taking a can of four star with her, to feed them, leaving me alone in the cafeteria with lots of riders who I didn't know and was unable to recognise because they all wore helmets with dark visors. I don't remember seeing them eat. Then Norman walked through the front door and I went to the toilet and when I came back the riders were sheep and I wasn't there but the cafeteria was and it was in a field where the sheep grazed and it all got too complicated and I woke up to find my hand immersed in a bowl of cold water.

'Pook!' I screamed almost immediately.

The room was dark. There was only the light from the landing lights of the building opposite, Fordie House, sneaking in from behind the closed curtains, and that didn't sneak in very far.

'Where are you? Come out!'

There was no answer and there was no sign of him.

'Meeoww!'

He crawled out from underneath the bed opposite. Jack was with him and his tongue was out.

'What the hell are you two doing in here?' I asked him.

'Ssshhh!' he went. 'Not so loud. She might hear you!'

'Who?'

'Ssshh!' he said, this time with his finger over his lips.

'Who?' I asked, whispering.

'Lucy,' he whispered at me in the dark.' She's here.'

'Where?'

'In the guest room. Mum let her stay.'

'Aha!' said I, rubbing my eyes. Poor Pook. That explained why he was taking refuge in my room. The Guest Room was next to his. Undoubtedly she would be prowling around the corridors in the early hours of the morning. He must have come into my room from the roof.

'Why the water?'

'What happened?'

'What do you mean what happened?'

'What happened today, on the bike?'

I had to tell him everything. Every single detail. Not a minute of the day could be omitted without him knowing what it was like. When I had finished, he was fast asleep on the bed and I was wide awake. Lucy was also wide awake, unless she was sleep walking. I fell asleep later on, much later on, just when everyone else was waking.

Over the next few days a casual interest in motor-cycling blossomed into a full-scale passion. No longer a passive and timid pillion passenger, I found extreme enjoyment in the competitive aspect of riding around on the roads, which was a good thing because there was no other aspect in a working day to find amusement in apart from what happened after hours. We'd race just about anything we could find, Police included. (This happened only once and that was in an area of Barnes that Chopper knew; an area of narrow footpaths and cul-de-sacs.) By the end of the week I was hooked, I was in love (Oh, sweet, sweet Kath) and had an appointment with the bank manager. I went there on Friday morning.

9

He was a bugger and a buggerer. That much was evident the moment I was led into his office by a rather epicene young gentleman with a bottle-blonde fringe feathered hair-cut. His name was Wild; he ignored me but looked lustily at my guide as I was shown to my seat. He dabbed at his nose with a soiled white handkerchief and followed the boy out with his eyes until the door was shut gently and then he shifted his eyes my way. Then he shifted his head to follow his eyes and his eyes followed his eyebrows up, then down. I felt like I was being undressed.

'Mmmmh,' said Mr Wild. 'I understand you want to apply for a bank loan, Mr . . . mmmh?'

He looked at the form, lying on the desk in front. 'Ah yes. Montgommery, isn't it?'

'It is,' I said.

'Montgommery. Yes, of course. And for what purpose do you want the money for this . . . *loan*?'

'I'd like to buy a . . .'

There was an eruption from across the desk as Wild emptied the contents of his nose in his handkerchief. When he had finished wiping his nose, I finished my sentence.

'I see,' he said, but he clearly didn't because he asked me the same questions after clearing his throat. Only this time turned an ear my way and bent a little closer in order to hear the response.

'A bike,' I said once more.

'Not for fifteen hundred pounds surely, Mr Montglomerate!'

'Montgommery,' I said.

'Quite,' he said. He was leaning forward, creeping across the table slowly enveloping everything that he came across. Before he came to me he retreated to his handkerchief and I witnessed another eruption.

He explained to me that he had hay fever and I explained to him the reasons for buying a motor-cycle. There was only one. The earning potential. It was not the one that enticed me but it was the only one I could tell them about. He didn't seem very excited about it until I mentioned that a brand new set of leathers would be necessary. Then he said the bank would consider the offer providing my parents signed the forms he gave me and I came back to show him the leathers. We shook hands and I left.

That evening I arrived home on time. In fact I was five minutes early. My mother was busy preparing herself in the bathroom as I walked in. My father was asleep in the lounge.

'Evening Dad!' I said. There was no reply. I walked along the hall. 'Evening Mum! Have a good day?'

She couldn't reply as she was in the final stages, the critical stage of her make-up application. The foundation had been applied, so had the powder, the rouge, the mascara, the false eyelashes, the hairnet, the hairspray, the ear-rings, the eye-liner, the nail-varnish and now, approximately one and a half hours after entering the bathroom, she was glossing her lips. I stood smiling in the doorway of the bathroom. I would have entered the bathroom but I didn't have an aqualung and the pungent aroma of all those hairsprays, hair-fixatives and scented perfumes could have wiped out a colony of blue-bottles.

Pook came skittering down the hall. He was with Jack; I cornered him and questioned him. Did he know where they were going? He did. Was he going to tell me? Yes, but only for a price. All right, was she in a good mood? Yes, she was. How about him? So was he.

I let him go and he ran off down the hall in the direction of the lounge. I heard a different programme on the television; then I heard my father moaning, then I heard him shouting. He wasn't in a good mood any more. I wasn't going to ask him for a signature this evening.

Mother had finished doing her lipstick and was looking in the mirror trying to decide what else she could put on her face in order to disguise the cruel fact that age had caught up with her mind and overtaken her body. She saw me watching her in the mirror.

'What is it, James?'

'You look lovely this evening, Mother.'

'Thank you. You're home early.'

'Well, I've been thinking about what you've been saying and . . .'

'Yes?'

'Well, you're right, and I'm wrong and I want to apologise.'

I dropped my head and looked at the carpet.

'Ah, that's awfully sweet of you, dear.'

She turned and smiled at me and I still kept my head low and servile looking, my face a perfect picture of misery.

'Do you want a hand there, Mother?' I said, lifting my head and smiling weakly.

She did, and I gave her one, but I was careful. I kept the other one free to hold my nose. She sprayed some more hairspray, pinned some more pins and told me that my dinner was in the oven.

I pulled out my dinner from the incinerator, played tiddlywinks with the Goulash and went ten rounds with the potato. Then Mother came in to say she was going.

'The meal was lovely, Mum. It really was.'

'That's sweet of you, darling.'

I got up from the bench and pecked her on the cheek. Now was the time to strike.

'Oh Mum,' I said, looking as innocent and spontaneous

as possible. This consisted of opening my eyes till they were the size of eggs. 'Could you sign this form I've got from the bank? It's nothing much.'

'I've got to go, darling. I haven't got a pen on me. I must rush.'

'I've got a pen, here.'

I pulled one out from my shirt pocket and gave it to her.

'What is this thing?' she said scribbling her name.

'It's a form of sponsorship, like those walks we do at school.'

'For charity?'

'Yes, that sort of thing.'

She signed the form and hobbled away down the hall on her high heels. One down, one to go, I thought.

I cornered my father the following day, just before I was leaving the house on the way to meet Chopper to see West Ham play their last game of the season. He was quite approving of the scheme mentioning that it was good to get into debt – everybody was.

With both forms signed, I hid them; put on my great-coat and headed off to West Ham.

10

The greatcoat wasn't such a great coat. In fact it's pretty terrible as coats go. It is about as heavy as the Combat Pack strapped to the rear of a Royal Marine, and it is made of material that provides a fair impression of what it must feel like to be a dog and have fleas. The saving grace, if you can call it that (I wouldn't; but as I haven't another coat, I will), is the ability the coat has for keeping a boy dry and that day, like most other days, it rained.

I went on the District Line to Upton Park. It was like travelling in a sardine can full of big-booted piranhas. The closer the train moved to the destination, the fuller the train became. This had its advantages and disadvantages. When the train was empty, there was more space to move and to sit, and to breathe. But you were unable to do any of these things due to a paralysis through fear. When the other elements in the carriage weren't playing cricket using beer bottles as balls, they were busy rediscovering their primeval instincts, swinging from one handrail to another, from one seat to the next, singing evil tunes, or stomping their extra-strong, extra-large booties in rhythm to just about anything except the tune being sung. And there was no point in moving to another carriage because exactly the same ritual was being performed in every carriage on the train. I was trapped. As the train filled, the noise grew. People sang anything; but no two people sang the same. That would have been defeatist. The object of the exercise was to make more noise and more flying saliva bombs then your opponent, the man next to you, or the granny lying underfoot.

At Upton Park, the train emptied itself of most of its people. Indeed, it emptied itself of most of its contents as well, the supporters having ripped up the seats and carried them off the train to use as portable umbrellas. The rain fell. I was the last off the train. I was just in time to see the pack surge down the platform screaming like wild dogs. They left the platform awash with paper cups, beer bottles, beer cans, confectionery wrappers, newspapers and the odd body or two badly trampled in the stampede. At the other end, by the ticket barrier, the two ticket collectors had locked and bolted themselves inside their booths, having given up any idea of collecting anything – other than a black eye – that might suggest that the supporters had paid for the privilege of travelling on the London Underground.

The ticket barrier looked like it had been struck by a human hurricane. When I walked through there was no sign of the smiling ticket collector who is normally there to greet and abuse the impoverished and inconvenienced traveller. This was a good thing, as I had skipped the barrier at Sloane Square, and worried about the excuse I was to give to the ogre at the other end for the length of the journey. This was on top of wondering whether the tribe of marauding Neanderthals had reached a sufficient stage in their development to want to make a human sacrifice to whatever god it was that patronised West Ham. (Whoever he was I'm pretty sure he wore extra-strong, extra-large Doc Martens, and with the celestial equivalent of a tattoo on his forehead. One that, more likely than not, said WEST HAM in enormous green letters.) Chopper was waiting outside the station and so were a couple of his friends.

'You made it then,' he said. 'We thought you wasn't coming.'

'I nearly didn't,' I said. 'I thought about crossing the footbridge and catching the next train back.'

'Oh yeah? Why didn't ya?'

'Another train came in from the opposite direction with twice the number of supporters.'

'You got nothing to worry about from them, they're pussycats – after all you support West Ham, Don't ya?'

'I do. But how do *they* know that?'

'Get a scarf. Wrap it round your neck and show 'em. Probably better, in fact, not to wrap it round your neck, but put it on your arm. In case some geezer strangles you. Anyway, this is 'arry . . .' 'arry and I shook hands – 'And this is Mick.' Mick and I shook hands.

'arry was shorter and much stockier than either Chopper or Mick; Mick was taller than Chopper and thinner – his arms were like thin sticks, and his head was a scaled down and scarred version of a railway map of Clapham Junction. 'arry's arms were covered in muscles and then covered with tattoos. All three had approximately no hair and egg shaped skulls. The uniform was the same for the three of them and just about every other skinhead wandering about the place. It was their battle gear, a combat US Airforce flight jacket, skintight jeans, and immaculate, shiny, extra-strong, extra-large booties. I said I was pleased to meet them. I did not get the impression that the feeling was mutual. We set off for the ground. They set off and I walked behind. The ground was packed.

It was probably a good game, it sounded like it; but you couldn't see much. In fact you couldn't see anything, and anything you did see was nothing to do with the game. The real game it seemed, was playing up on the terraces between rival factions of supporters trying to outdo each other in psychopathic behaviour. A pitched battle started about halfway through the first half. Beer bottles and darts were the most popular form of missile and these were thrown like grenades, lobbed up and over the partitioning fence to bounce off the thick skulls, tempered over the years with much use as dangerous weapons and body-shields, and sodden in alcohol. This had an equal and opposite reaction, setting off a return salvo that did exactly the same; and the process went on and on until the pitched battle spread onto the pitch, stopping the game until the mounted policemen had rounded up the culprits, smacked their wrists a few times and marched them out of the ground. At half-time, the score wasn't a score: it was nothing-nothing. We thought about going to buy some hot dogs but the thought only remained a thought because we were unable to get through the sea of supporters.

Just before the second half was due to get under way, Chopper pointed out a phenomenon that a person is only likely to see at a football match. It is a game played by many but only accomplished by a few. The target is simple and blue and is normally seen on the head of a policeman; it is his hat. The idea is to kidnap it. When this is accomplished, and it's not accomplished that often, the proud owner will then run around in front of the stands parading his trophy to the adoring and hysterical fans until he is caught, his wrists are smacked and he is led away. The truly gifted hatnappers don't get caught. They dive into the stands, chased by policeman, and disappear with their trophy. I saw one make a clean getaway. The other three attempts ended face down in the mud and the rain, secured by two policeman. Eventually the second half started.

After many more bottle barrages, fist fights, and hatnapping attempts the ref blew the final whistle. The final score went in favour of the police in the terraces and a draw on the field.

Outside we were walking down the street in a swarm of supporters escorted by the police.

'What did you think of the game?' Chopper asked.

'Which one?'

'Both.'

I told him that I didn't think that the football was as entertaining as the crowd and he agreed, though he didn't look very happy about it and neither did his friends.

We headed north on the street towards Upton Park tube station. The sun was low in the sky and reflected itself in the shop windows on the right-hand side of the street as a brilliant orange orb and the many youngsters ran happily waving their scarves. But on most of the faces of the supporters was a look of disappointment, as if not enough had happened. We didn't reach the station.

The missiles came at us in beautiful and well-measured lobs, delivered from a distance of about twenty yards by a hidden bunch of Arsenal supporters that appeared from behind a street corner, ahead. They lined up in ranks, fired their projectiles and scurried away before most of the bottles and bricks had reached the target zone. They worked on the same principle as the US Air Force used when dropping the atomic bomb on Hiroshima. The bomb was dropped but the effects of the explosion were not felt until the combat crews were well out of reach. The core of the explosion took place in the centre of the pack about twenty feet in front of us. Everybody immediately took cover if they could find some, and took a battering if they couldn't. Mick couldn't. A rogue glass bottle struck him just above the groin area. He went down onto the pavement groaning and clutching his stomach. Chopper went down with him.

The effects of the blast were twofold. It made more work for the street cleaners and provoked frenzied cries for retaliation. The police were powerless to stop the now mad, rabid and bloodthirsty crowd. They could have

tried but the losses would have been appalling. One bright
spark, a young lad with a ruddy complexion and too many
tattoos running at the front of the pack backwards yelled.

'Do you want to look like a 'uckin' 'unt?'

There was a whole lot of howling. Obviously everybody
did.

The pack started to run at full speed. We were with them,
having left Mick sitting on the curb amongst the rubble,
recuperating. We rounded the corner scattering pedestrians, motorists and shopkeepers busy trying to shut their
shops. Ahead of us, at the end of the street, were the pack of
jeering Arsenal supporters.

They started screaming all sorts of pervy things in uni-
son. These boys were all brain surgeons specialising in pre-
frontal lobotomies.

Not to be deterred, the pack chased them down the street.
I chased them as far as the train station and then decided
that I didn't have much quarrel or indeed much enthusiasm
for spending the rest of the afternoon hunting and kicking
Arsenal supporters. I thought I'd go home and see Marie.
Perhaps she could be persuaded to come over to the flat and
call us her 'leetle devils'.

Unfortunately, just as I was about to disappear into the
warm, lighted and dry interior of the train station, old
Chopper turns around and sees me hovering near the
entrance. He was mad, all right, you could see it in his eyes.
They were bulging in their sockets in anticipation.

He shouted back at me, above the noise of the stamped-
ing crowd.

'C'mon Jimbo, we're goin' to kill 'em!'

I had half a mind to tell him I had to get home before tea.
But it was worry of losing the other half that stopped me
from doing so. I didn't say anything.

'You ain't chicken, are ya?'

'No.'

'Good. I can't staand chickens.'

He meant it. I think he would have wrung my neck and sold me to Sainsbury's if he thought I was. As an illustration of my faith, courage, and blind stupidity I ran off down the street in pursuit of the pack. This is the way I always ended up in trouble. The reason for being thrown, sometimes bodily, from the closed doors of honourable learning establishments.

11

Well, it wasn't long before we were travelling in the van, locked up, just me and about twenty others. I didn't really want to attract much attention so I sat over in a corner with my coat wrapped tight. The others – they were so happy, even those that had torn faces and bloody noses; they sang and cracked jokes and one man, who was maybe forty, told a joke about the reason for policemen having pointed hats. He said it was because they had pointed heads. Now I didn't think that was funny but the rest of them – they howled. Chopper did, too. Then, they sang the song about never walking alone with the chorus going, 'You'll nehhver walk alone, you'll never walk alone.' And they must have been singing at the tops of their voices, I sort of sang as well – though I had to fake a good bit of it as I didn't know the words – and whilst I was singing away, the partition opened up and this face shouted,

'You'll never walk again, mate, let alone walk alone, if you don't quit makin' that *racket!*'

For saying that, the policeman was rewarded, sort of, with some filthy language being shouted at him from the rear and also a stream of saliva. Most of it came from this little boy, about eleven – no older than Pook – who had freckles, short hair and boots that laced half way to his groin. They were enormous, these boots. I don't know how he managed to be such a good spitter; he could shoot five – one directly after the other and all deadly accurate. Everybody in the whole van, except of course the two policemen driving, laughed, and I must say that I joined in with them. The hatch was slammed to and a cheer went up.

I was starting to worry a little now. Going to jail was going to make the fossils terribly mad, even though I didn't do anything wrong apart from run along in the streets with the crowd. Proving that I had nothing to do with it was going to take some sharp talk.

After about ten minutes the van arrived in a courtyard, having come through Plaistow, and we were unloaded.

'C'mon you animals,' said the guard. 'Out you get, chop-chop!'

Chop-chop everyone said, chop-chop. We got out of the van chop-chop and were led up some back stairs to the entrance on the first floor. The guard was up ahead and I was walking up behind Chopper when suddenly this guard was hit on the back, on the cap, and finally as a testament to perseverance – on the neck. I felt something move behind me and when I turned, the little boy, very serious, gave me a scalding look. He had a nerve, an awful nerve.

'All right then,' said the guard, after all the skinheads had quietened down their laughing. 'Which one of you was responsible?'

Nobody said anything; it was so quiet you could hear yourself breathe and all the time the guard stood still just staring at us; an awful cold stare it was, too. Then, he said, looking at me, 'You did it, didn't ya? Come here.'

'Me?' I said, a little quacky.

'You . . . Come here.'

I walked up, slowly, feeling all nervous.

'Why d'you do it? Think it's funny did ya? It's not is it?'

'Nope.'

He had started to slap his cosh in his hand and I was starting to shake, a bit.

'So why did you do it, eh?'

'I . . . I didn't,' I stammered.

'You didn't, eh,' he said, slowly and quietly. 'So who did then? Who was responsible?'

Well, now he had his head tilted over and was slapping that cosh with all sorts of vigour and I didn't like it one bit. I would have given anything, right then, to have been at home helping our French bittie make the dinner. I thought he was going to do some rearranging, put the old ear in a position that was not normal. He didn't though. Some fat skinhead yelled out.

'I'm responsible.' So we all looked down at him and the policeman smiled. But before the policeman had a chance to beckon the skinhead up the stairs, he added, 'I knows it. Me mum told me I was.'

This made all the other skinheads scream with laughter, they roared, and one after the other all admitted that they were also responsible. The poor policeman had to give up. With me at the front, we were led inside.

It was dark inside and we were led along a couple of corridors before we came to the cells, then we were separated into groups of six and locked up. The jail stank of beer and upchuck. Some of the cells were filled with West Ham supporters and some cells had Arsenal men in them. They were all singing and seemed very happy after all the trouble at the ground; but there was one man who alone managed to douse every drunken voice in the cells nearby and he sang,

'Scotland, Scotland, we love you Scotland!'

We had passed him on the way in. He was wrapped in a tartan banner and slumped up against the cell wall, blubbering. He must have been drinking an awful amount to have been in the state he was in.

'Shut up!' the guard shouted. For some reason that I didn't understand, the others quietened – but not the Scot. He stopped singing, burped, started swearing about filthy British beer, stopped doing that, and then launched himself into, 'Wemmbelleee! Wemmbellee! We're goin' to

Wemblee and we're goin' to win the cup! Wemmbellee! . . .' etc.

The guard walked back down the corridor, towards where the Scot was. All of us in the cell gathered around to watch.

'Shut it!' the guard cried.

'Ooooh,' came the response from most of the prisoners. The guard carried on walking and drew his cosh.

'Wemmbellee! Wemmbellee! We're goin' to Wemmbellee and we're goin' to win the cup!' etc.

The guard didn't say anything else until he walked past our cell and got three in the face from the gobber that had been locked up with us. I didn't even see the little boy do it until it was over and I was being stared at by the guard as he came towards our cell.

When he unlocked the cell door we were all sitting placidly on the bunks and the stone floor, trying to look as innocent as possible. I was twiddling my thumbs and finding it very difficult to swallow – being scared and everything.

'All right you bastards, I know it's one of you six. Now which . . .'

He was interrupted by: 'My bonneeee lies overrr the ocean. My bonneee lies over the . . .'

'*Shut up!*' the guard screamed.

'. . . sea.'

A toothless skinhead, sitting opposite me in a corner started sniggering. I knew he shouldn't have done that with that guard being as mad as he was, and sure enough the guard comes charging in and slaps him one across the skull.

'You think it's funny do ya?' the guard asked. 'Do ya? Well tell me then, bright boy, how funny *this* is.'

He smacked him again, this time a backhander. It must have hurt like a bastard, but that skinhead didn't make a sound.

'Who did it then?' he asked me.

Only then did it come to me why he was always asking me

and never any of the others. You see, I was dressed differently and he thought, most likely, that if he asked me, I'd get awfully scared and tell him all he wanted to know – once he'd started flashing that truncheon of his. I was properly tempted to tell him, not wishing to be on the receiving end of that cosh, but I sort of admired the little boy's nerve, no matter what a bad thing it was, and so I kept quiet.

The Scot didn't. He started blabbing some Gaelic song that none of us could understand and the guard got very annoyed and rushed out of our cell to shut him up. I breathed more easily when he went, because I wasn't sure that I'd keep my mouth shut once he started on me, if he did.

We heard a tussle going on in the Scot's cell and then the guard said:

'That'll teach ya. You rotten drunken Scottish hooligan.'

Then we heard the door shut and the guard walk away and no sooner had the guard gone a couple of paces, than the Scot started up once more.

'Mggengleee! Mggengleee! Wig owin' ooh Meggengleee ing wig owin ogg' in' icup!'

As the guard walked past our cell, now smirking, the little boy leapt to his feet and would have rushed to the window to spit if Chopper hadn't tripped him up and told him to shut up and sit down. The guard walked away and just as he was about to shut the cell corridor door behind him, the Scot, who must have wriggled out of his gag, shouted:

'Waiter! More beer!' The door closed.

In our cell someone asked, 'What time is it?'

'Time I was out of 'ere,' said Chopper. 'I 'ate these places.'

'How long are we going to have to stay here?' I asked.

''till someone bails you out.'

'Who?'

'Don't matter – as long as they got some money.'

'Who's going to bail you out?'

'Sherry. She ain't going to be too pleased about it neither.'

'How does she know you're here.'

'She don't until they charge me, then I call her up.'

We didn't get a chance to make any phone calls for a couple of hours and by that time it was seven. I'd tried to think of somebody other than the fossils who I could call but as I was only allowed one phone call and I wasn't sure if my uncle or any of my aunts would be in, I called home. Luckily I spoke to Pook and when I told him what had happened he just said, 'They're going to kill you James, I know it.'

Well, I left the message with him and settled back in the cell sitting on the old greatcoat, and waited. A lot of the cells had emptied by eight and once, about eight thirty, I watched this fight in the cell opposite. There were two men squabbling over a cigarette butt, when one of them says, 'You touch that and I swear I'll kick every tooth loose in your 'ead.' Then they start a furious scrap – rolling over and over as they were banging and punching each other. Finally the taller of the two gets his man in a headlock and instead of just making him submit like we do at school, he starts banging the head down on the stone floor. Up and down, up and down the head went. Chopper loved it and was shouting all sorts of encouragement at the smaller man and when it was over he simply said, 'He did all right,' and went back to his bunk. The police took no notice and we didn't do much talking after that, though I did find out that the little boy's name was Johnny Reggae.

12

'Montgommery?' said the guard. 'Your mother's 'ere.'

By this time Chopper was fuming on account of Sherry's lack of appearance and he said, 'Montgommerwee, Montgommerwee? Who is Montgommerwee?'

The guard told him to be quiet and Chopper swore at him.

'I'll see you later,' said the guard.

'Promises, promises,' said Chopper and Mick, who had been lying quiet on the top bunk nursing his wound, started haw-hawing until he discovered it was too painful and so stopped.

Did she look angry! She looked ready to kill. I tried smiling but she bore a pretty icy gaze that didn't warm much. Pook was smiling, though, and Jack wagged his tail.

''ere 'e is Mrs Montgommery,' said the guard as he led me up to the desk. Mother thanked him and whilst the counter partition was opened, a couple of forms were presented for mother to sign, which she did, huffing and puffing all the time and making sure I knew she wasn't in the best of moods.

'Has he ever been in trouble before, Mrs Montgommery?' asked the desk sergeant.

'No . . . never,' said old Mother, trying to hold back the tears. I could see she was all emotional about everything and I knew I'd let her down again; but as far as I knew I hadn't done anything wrong: I didn't fight, I didn't throw anything, nothing like that – I just ran with the crowd.

Pook kept trying to catch my eye to show me that he thought it was funny, but I didn't look at him.

'What am I being charged with?' I asked, and just as I did so the door to the police station was flung open, and in walked a skinhead of the feminine variety – same clothes, same boots, same hair, except the haircut had a tail of hair that hung from the base of her head. This girl stomped up to the counter and said,

'You holdin' me boyfriend?'

Mother stepped back a pace and Pook asked me who it was and I had to tell him that I didn't know.

'Who is your boyfriend?' said the desk sergeant.

'Chopper 'arris.'

'Arfur 'arris you mean?'

'That's 'im.'

So this was Sherry, I was thinking. Mother looked on, not quite believing what her eyes showed her and all of us listened as the skinhead and the desk sergeant argued over the price of Chopper's bail. Half-way through and Mum turns to me and says,

'Is this the boy you used to work with?'

I said: 'Chopper? Yes, I work with him.'

'*Used to*, James.'

'No, and I'm not going to argue,' said I, thinking it was better to let her cool down for a while.

'We'll see about that.'

It was then that I was sure we were going to have one God almightily huge argument when we got through the door at number four. There was a terrible storm brewing, and I knew it.

'. . . and,' continued the desk sergeant, looking like he was enjoying himself, 'we suspect that your dearly beloved Arfa' might also be leader of the gang responsible for the vandalism and violence that occurred during and after today's game. Unprovoked attacks on members of the public; wanton destruction of public and private property. There are a number of other charges all of which I can list if you wish, and all of which contribute to the sum asked for his bail.'

'Did you hear that, James?' said Mother. 'Vandalism and violence – how disgusting!'

'It is, Mum, but it wasn't like that.'

'I'm shocked!' said Mum.

'That's cobblers,' the little skinhead girl said. 'You're just trying to wind me up.'

'Mr 'arris is a 'ooligan. We know it, you know it and now Mr Montgommery knows it . . .'

'I don't,' said I.

'Shut up, James,' said Mother. So I did.

'As I was saying,' continued the desk sergeant. 'If it weren't for your boyfriend's shall we say anarchistic tendencies . . .'

'You can say what you want, mate. I know 'e ain't no queer.'

'If you'd kindly *shut up* and let me finish.'

'Right, go ahead,' said the skinhead.

'If it weren't for his . . . er . . . 'ooliganistic tendencies, Mr Montgommery 'ere, a boy who has previously had no trouble with the law, should not be 'ere today. Isn't that right Mrs Montgommery?'

'That is correct, Inspector,' said mother, trying to flatter him. He smiled.

'What you bi'n tellin' 'im, then?' asked the skinhead.

'Nothing.' I said.

'So why's 'e saying that Chopper's to blame for you's be'n 'ere, if you said nuffin'?'

'I don't know.'

'How 'bout you then? Wot' chew bin tellin' 'im?'

'None of your business,' said Mum, looking a little bit flustered.

'That's where you're wrong, see,' said Sherry. 'It's always me business when 'e's in trouble; 'coz it's me, like, that has to come an' get 'im aart. I 'ave to pay 'is bail and when '*u* start tellin' the copper 'ere fings that ain't true '*e* puts the bail up. Don't you, doll?'

The desk sergeant sighed. 'The bail is determined by the severity of the crime committed. Now I've told you the price; if you're going to pay, give me the money. Otherwise, get out – I have work to do.'

Sherry gave him the money and a guard was sent off to get Chopper.

'Will that be all with us, Inspector?' said Mum and the sergeant said that he thought so; all charges (I still didn't know what they were) would 'most likely' be dropped. Mother thought this was magnificent and she was 'so happy' that I wouldn't have a criminal record for the rest of my life. I wouldn't have anyway but it would have done no good to have told her that – not at that time. So, we were just about to leave, mother completely 'over the moon' at the sergeant's kindness of heart and generosity of spirit, when Chopper comes screaming down the corridor, swearing his head off and holding his nose. I didn't know what in the world was up with him but when I saw him, his face all bloodied, and struggling with the guard, I knew this was going to give her all the fuel she wanted for her fire.

It was such bad timing. If he'd come down two minutes later we'd have been outside and undoubtedly arguing. As it was, I could do no more than shake my head.

'He had a slight accident, Sarge. He tripped up – those big boots, tsk tsk tsk tsk, much too big for you boy, no good for walking in eh?'

Mother watched as Chopper spat a bit of blood and then laughed. After, he said:

'Wanker.'

'What d'you say boy?' the guard asked.

'You 'eard.'

'I think it's time you learnt some manners, boy,' said the guard, all smiley now.

That Chopper – he was looking at a lot of trouble and that fat lip of his was going to earn him some hell of a hiding.

'I think it's time we left,' said mother.

'Yeah, go on then,' said Sherry. 'Bugger off.'

And at the same time I heard Chopper start arguing with the guard. My friend was furious and would have started to fight if his hands had not been handcuffed. Mother watched all of this, her mouth open.

'James, Pook, come with me!' she said after a while.

It would have been much better for us if I could have gone but it just didn't seem right to walk out now, seeing how things were between my friend and the guard. So I asked the guard why he hit Chopper and pretended not to have heard her command. The guard didn't answer immediately, looking first at the desk sergeant and then at Chopper. Then he said that Chopper had tried to hit him.

'But didn't you just say that he had tripped?' I asked.

'That's right,' said the guard. 'He tripped when he tried to have a go at me.'

'James, *come on!*' said Mother.

Chopper called him a liar and the guard told him to shut it; then they started pushing each other and Sherry joined in, screaming, 'You leave him alone, you fascist bastard,' and the desk sergeant had to stop it all by putting an armlock on Chopper and pressing his head onto the counter; so his nose was squashed in the wood top.

'Now then,' the desk sergeant said, 'take it easy. I don't want any trouble from you. Any more outbreaks like this, Arfa', and you won't being going home for a while. Understand?'

It looked mightily uncomfortable having your arm up by your ear and with your nose squashed and everything; but old Chopper took it all without wincing; he said nothing and when he was asked again, 'Understand?' he nodded.

'James, *come on!*'

'Is there anything I can do?' I said and Chopper said, 'Nothing,' but the desk sergeant added that he thought I might be needed as a witness for the prosecution and I said I wouldn't do it as there was nothing to say that was done and was wrong.

'You will, James,' Mother said.

'No, I won't.'

'You will if I say you will,' she said.

'I won't.'

'We'll call you, Mrs Montgommery,' said the desk sergeant, and out we went.

13

I think 'Why did you do it?' was the first question and if it wasn't that it was 'You know you will be branded as a criminal for the rest of your life; a son of ours – a common thief. How will we live it down?' And if it wasn't either of those two little gems it was something along the lines of my lack of responsibility, my unwillingness to grow up, a terrible choice of friends, a 'frightful example to your younger brother', a 'positively unhealthy attitude towards life, morals,' etc., etc., and all of this said at once and at random by both parents in no particular order but said simultaneously; hence the confusion.

We had been sitting in the kitchen for about an hour or so interrupted every now and then by Pook. He'd come in and say that Arabella was on the phone, or Prue, or Lucy, and each time he poked his head through the door he'd be very solemn and serious when delivering the message but would sneak a grin or a wink at me before closing the door; and up mother would get – so distraught, so brave – answering the telephone in a jolly voice with not a hint of despair. And in the meantime, Dad and I sat on opposite sides of the table, him shaking his head slowly from side to side and me fidgeting and picking my nose, until Mum returned – funereal, a tear or two ready to drop, clutching a box of tissues, and on we'd go, around and around in circles.

'. . . and if you are lucky, fingers crossed, the Inspector says you might get away without a conviction, Oh God, I hope so. You fool, you fool, James. I knew we shouldn't have let him do this, George. I had a feeling right from the start and I said so, didn't I? Didn't I say so, George?'

'You did, dear.'

'And now look what has happened. A complete and utter disaster. What are we to do? What *are* we to do?'

Here, I'd explain, again, that there was no disaster: I would not get convicted; nothing wrong had been done; we were simply protecting ourselves, etc., etc., and all of this would be swept aside and ignored.

'. . . and what a hooligan that boy is! Did you see what he did to that poor guard? Why he tried to attack him. The boy is an animal, he really is . . .'

Here I'd try to interrupt to point out that neither myself nor herself saw the incident that the guard claimed had occurred. But the attempt was futile and after trying it twice I gave up and adopted the policy of nodding.

In the end, two and a half hours after the beginning, old mumma said that if I didn't 'shape up' I'd have to 'ship out'. This sounded like the first bit of sense that had been spoken all evening, and after they had all gone to bed I went up on the roof and thought it through.

The only problem with moving out was finding a place to live. With both the bank forms signed, money would not be a problem as the motor-cycle would pay for the rent, (I kept as quiet as a dead man about my job and the bank loan), and so, at one in the morning when I snuck back down the pipe I had an idea that I'd be leaving, though I didn't know where I'd be going nor when.

14

I went up to Hyde Park on Sunday after going down to the
Golden Duck to shoot a couple of Invader games. The
park was packed and there were no ducks. I looked everywhere. Up by the cafeteria, under the bridge, even down in
Kensington Gardens; but they weren't anywhere to be
seen. I asked one of the park-keepers, 'Where are the
ducks?' but he didn't seem to know and so in the end I
gave up.

I was standing on the bridge looking down at the boats,
at the people rowing. Always there was a man and a
woman and if he wasn't busy showing her his Olympic
speed, he was illustrating how wonderful he was at standing up. Now I know that standing up doesn't sound like so
much of a great thing – and it shouldn't – but the girls!
They went a little bit sick when such heroic feats of courage were displayed, laughing like they'd never seen anything so funny. It was a pretty lonesome sight.

On the grass in the middle of the park, people
smooched. Oily bellies rolling round on a towel, like
beasts do in a field. You couldn't miss seeing these things.
People were at it all over the park: in the lee of big elms;
out in the flat cut grass; some were at it on the park bench.
Old couples, young couples, foreign, English – they were
all there and they were all doing it, and I thought that the
sun works in strange ways, growing things.

I was suffering, too, from this heat problem and zipped
out the park to make a phone-call. Her name being
Angelica.

'Hallo, is Angelica there, please?' said I.

Unfortunately her mother answered and when I told her who it was that was calling she put the phone down. I tried a couple of other numbers, but there was no answer. The last number I tried belonged to a girl who went to my last school. Her name was Joan; she was a studious type and not the best of company to laugh with. She took an awful lot of coaxing and pleading with to get out of the house, but I did it, and I met her at three o'clock under Bowater House. 'I can only come out for an hour, James,' she had said. I wasn't expecting any miracles.

She turned up twenty minutes late wearing a tartan skirt and a blouse and green pumps.

'How are you?' I said.

'All right.'

'You look great, you really do.'

'Thank you.'

We smiled.

'Come, let's find the ducks.'

And so off we went, with me doing most of the talking. We walked around the Serpentine, in the sun, to where the boats were moored and I rented us a row boat. I was a hell of an oarsman, I really was, and before we had cleared the dock I'd hit four boats.

'Are you enjoying yourself, Joan?' I asked when we had finally made it to the middle of the lake.

'No.'

'Good, good,' and we rowed on.

We rowed purposefully, mostly in circles collecting the oars that kept disappearing over the side, and sometimes, when the going was really good, we went in a straight line.

Joan did not look happy and so, for her entertainment, I stood up and rocked the boat. It was peculiar – she didn't laugh. I rocked the boat with more vigour. She still had a stony face. So I gave it everything and she got soaked.

'You stupid fool,' she shouted at me. 'Look what you've done – you've ruined my dress! Just ruined it. I hate you!'

'I was only trying to cheer you up. I didn't mean to get you wet. I'm sorry.'

'Take me in!'

So I rowed her back, hitting a few more boats on the way in, much to Joan's embarrassment and when we were walking back she apologised and I suggested that we have tea. I felt terrible about her dress – so I bought the tea.

'When are your exams?' I asked.

'About a month. When are yours?'

'I'm not sure,' said I, trying to evade the question. Success.

'Well, mine are next month – I'm taking Maths, Physics and Chemistry, you know . . .'

'I didn't know that.'

'Well I am and if I do well in these, and I think I will you know because I've been working *so* hard, then I'll be set up for next term, and that's the A-level year, you know . . .'

'Right.'

'So then I'm going to work like an absolute dog, take my A's – and I think I'll get good grades in them and if they're as good as I think they will be, then I'll take Oxbridge.'

'Good,' I said.

'Then, of course there is the problem of what to study at Oxford. I mean I'm equally as good at Maths as I am at Physics, but I enjoy Chemistry the most. You see what I mean?'

'Yes.'

'So I'll have to make a decision over that soon. And it is most worrying. What do you think I should do?'

'Do the one you enjoy the most.'

'But it's not as easy as that, James, as I explained to you

just a minute ago. Now, I'll say it again. I'm *better* at Maths and Physics, but I *enjoy* Chemistry the most. You see?'

'Right.'

'So what should I do?'

'Do the one you enjoy the most.'

'Tsk, James! But I won't be as good at it.'

'Well what are you going to do afterwards – for a job?'

'After Oxford?' said Joan. Then she sipped her tea. Filthy stuff that it was. 'I'm going to post-graduate school.'

'How long will you be there?'

'I'm not sure. Three maybe four years and I might do *that* in America.'

'That's good. And how long does that mean you're going to be in school?'

'It's not *school*, James.'

'Well what is it then?'

'University.'

'What's the difference?'

'It's obvious.'

'It is?'

'Yes. One is called school and the other is called University.'

'They both sound the same to me,' I said. Then I drank some tea, and said, 'So how long will it be before you're out and working?'

'Nine, ten years, maybe more if I want. I could go on studying until I was thirty-five if I switched degrees and things.'

'That would be exciting,' said I with not much enthusiasm.

'Oh it would be.'

I was daring then – I lit up a cigarette. Took two good smokes.

'I didn't know you smoked, James.'

'I don't. You make me nervous.'

'Do I?'

'Yes.'

'Oh.'

Well, then we sat for a bit, out on the grass, in the two chairs, looking at the boats floating around and all the people walking about. It was quite fine sitting in the sun.

'What are you going to do this summer?' I said.

'Study. How 'bout you?'

I told her about my job but she wasn't the sort of girl that liked that type of thing and soon the subject was back onto her academic career. She croaked on and on about it – how pleased her family were with her results, how they thought it was a splendid idea, blah, blah, blah. When four o'clock came I was a happy man. I walked her back to South Ken and when we got there and came to say goodbye, old Joan said I had been a great help (I'd said 'right' to everything she had said, answers *and* questions), and that she was sure I'd find another school for next term, and that she was sorry that she had to go back so early, but she had to do her revision.

'Right.'

'Poor James,' she said. 'I feel so sorry for you. It must be so traumatic to be expelled especially at such a critical stage in your academic career.'

'Right.'

'Poor James.'

Joan went up the stairs and opened her front door.

'Bye bye, James,' she said.

'Bye bye, Joan,' I said.

'Bye bye.'

'Bye bye.'

'Oh Joan,' I called, just as she was about to close her door.

'Yes?'

'I think we should talk Maths next time. I'm excellent with figures.'

'Okay,' she said and shut the door. I don't think she got the joke.

I got home that night feeling pretty miserable and as we weren't on speaking terms, I didn't have to eat dinner. I settled down in my room and read *Shogun*. Then I slept.

Monday was a good day on the bike. Chopper was happy because he felt he would not be going to court as he had found out on Saturday that some other 'geeza' had been collared as ring leader. We played Invader and I won. He did not like this. We also had a number of long jobs and I witnessed my first street fight – Chopper v. truck driver. Truck driver won and chased Chopper down the street bellowing and blubbering at him. Highly comical it was.

After work we were sitting in the pub near Rocket with our beer, and Chopper and my self were talking motorcycle talk, with him going through the list of all the most suitable bikes for the job and with me asking him about each. All of this needed to be said as I had come to the conclusion that I'd like to get a bike and work for the summer. As I had an American licence the capacity of the machine was not restricted. The money was: I had to put the five hundred that had been given to me over the years in gift money as collateral for the bank to give me a thousand. This left me thirteen hundred pounds, after insurance, to buy my machine. So these things were being said when in walked Frankie, Rita, the man I saw howling on the landing on the first day and the little beautiful girl from the cafeteria, Kath.

Holy moly, my heart started doing funny things when they came to our table. I couldn't look her way. I think it must have been the chemistry thing that you always hear about because I was feeling the peculiars all over when she came to sit down. My hands were jittery, my face lit up, I was fidgeting up and down the bar bench. I couldn't stop, no matter how hard I tried. She didn't say anything to me or look at me or anything – and she didn't have to for there was something mighty powerful at work.

'What d'you want to drink?' Frankie asked.

We said beer and so did Rita and the hairy man, who had been introduced as Norman, but K.k.kath (I write it that way because that is how it would have been said) wanted a gin and tonic. Frank went up to the crowded bar and Rita and Chopper started talking whilst Norman scratched his scalp. Then he scratched his arm, then the other arm, then his chest, then his stomach, then himself, then he was happy and grinned. I was looking at his face, noticing the little red goatee beard on his chin and how his hair was swept back in a pony tail and what big brown eyes he had, when Frank came back with the drinks, and put them down.

Well, he had just put them down and we were all taking them when Rita sent hers flying. She was showing with her hand exactly how nimble her Triumph was in the crowded traffic. Now, as the seating was arranged with me in the middle of Kath and Chopper, and her in the middle of me and Norman, I couldn't move anywhere in a hurry and neither could she and the problem was that all that beer came flooding down the table looking for a lap to soak.

As quick as a flash I had my trusty Barbour over her lap saving her dress as she started squealing and the beer started dripping. I got a lapful but it was worth it as she started gushing praise and thanks on my gallant soul. I was all chuffed.

In the meantime Chopper had also got a lapful. He was none to pleased about it and swore.

'I shouldn't do that if I were you, Chopper,' said Norman.

'What?' said Chopper.

'Argue. It's terrible for your bio-rhythms, man.'

'Has 'e bin' smokin', Rita?'

'No idea,' said Rita.

'Are you stoned, Norman?'

I don't think old Norman was listening. His eyes looked glazed over and his face was transfixed with a stupid grin as he tilted his head upwards, heavenwards, in search of divine inspiration. It came, eventually, as we waited with baited breath.

'No,' said Norman. Then he got up and ran off.

'Where did he go?' I asked.

'To the gents,' someone replied.

'Why did he run?'

'It's his guru – 'e feeds 'im curry. Poor bastard,' said Rita.

''e's a right smelly hippy,' said Chopper, into his beer.

'What time is it?' Kath asked and I told her it was seven fifteen. Then I got up to get a cloth to wipe down my lap and my coat. When I got back to the table Chopper and Kath were leaving. I gave her the crash-helmet and we arranged to meet the following morning, me and Chopper, and out they went. She did say goodbye.

''ere,' said Rita, sidling up close. 'You wanna buy some shit, man, eh? Coke, Smack, Speed, Dope, Amyl, Uppers, Downers, All-arounders – anything you want, man. I can get it. I'm your man. Listen I can also do you . . .'

And Rita rattled of a list of drugs that rivalled the Queen's speech in length and when she finished I told her that I was happy with the mug of beer in front so she offered her hand saying, 'Well it's nice to have ya aboard, James.'

'Thank you,' I said, and we shook. I thought I was going to black out – she had the grip of an ape – and whilst I was busy regaining consciousness, Norman returned, displaying all the visual characteristics a man might show after a night in the company of four skilled

Geisha girls (this I learnt from Shogun; what a life it is to be a Lord).

'Ah,' said Norman. 'That's better. Much better.'

Norman lifted his pint, adjusted his leg position and scratched his scalp – all at the same time. The beer went down, the leg crossed and I could have sworn it was Christmas, the amount of dandruff he let loose.

'The secret is to get it all out, everything. Know what I mean?' he said.

'I'm afraid I don't,' I said – though watching him scratch his skull gave a half-idea. He scratched it some more and went on to say, 'My theory is this: when a man, any man *or* woman for that matter, gets uptight, the cause is internal pressure. Am I right?'

Without waiting for a reply from Frank, myself or Rita, Norman went on: 'So, this pressure, a terrible pressure . . . a horribly crippling pressure . . .'

'Get on wid' ya,' said Rita.

'Well it builds up and up until the pressure is intolerable and unbear —'

'We've had that,' said Frank.

'I know, I know just let me tell me story will 'ya?'

'Get on with it, then,' said Rita.

'All right, man. All right. So, um . . . where was I?'

'A horribly crippling nasty boring pressure building up inside of ya'. Say, are you sure you ain't been smoking some of that weed, Norman?' said Rita.

'No, I've told you, Reeta. Now let me finish.'

'Should I get a drink now, before last orders, or wait until you finish?'

'Ha ha, you're funny Frank,' said Norman as he took another sip from his beer. 'So, the pressure is built up and your body can't take none of it because it's gotta get out, right?'

'Right, Norman,' said the others, looking vacantly out the window.

'So what's to be done with all this . . .'

'Pressure?' said Rita.

'Exactly,' said Norman.

'You get stoned, simple.'

'No,' said Norman, 'you do not get stoned, Rita. You go to the toilet and flush it out of your system. There! I bet you didn't know that!' said Norman triumphantly. He was very excited with this revelation and his special extra-strong Greek import worry beads jumped about on his chest whilst being secured to his neck, which was also jumping and jerking.

'Norman, are you sure you aren't constipated?' Frank asked.

'No, no. I'm being serious, Frank – perfectly serious. Conchita feels the same way . . .'

'Maybe Conchita's constipated, I wouldn't put it past her – not with all that health muck she eats,' said Rita.

'Rita, please,' said Norman. 'Don't wind me up. *Please*!'

'All right Norman. 'ave a drink. Don't get yourself into a fluster – we never see you no more. You're always in the company of the doyen of the men's urinal – Mr Armitage Shanks. Sit down and relax.'

Norman took a couple of deep breaths and then drank some beer.

'There, feeling better?' said Rita.

'Yes. Much, thank you.'

'Good, good.'

Then, just as Norman put glass to mouth Rita screamed, making Norman jump and Frank laugh. Norman put his glass down.

'I'm off then,' said Rita. 'Are you coming?'

'Not if Daisy's going to be there.'

'All right,' said Rita, and she got up and so did the table. Norman's drink ended up in Norman's lap. When Norman called her an elephant he obviously struck a nerve for her face dropped and the pub was suddenly quiet. Fortunately for Norman – though not the audience of sozzled businessmen who looked on in eager anticipation – Rita turned on her heel and left, slamming the door.

'Who's Daisy?' I asked after a while.

Frank started laughing.

'Daisy's Rita's boyfriend and founder of The Grave-diggers. 'e's strange,' said Norman.

'How is he strange?'

'You'll find out.'

'Well why don't you like him?'

'Because he teases me.'

''e don't tease you,' said Frank. 'Daisy don't tease anyone – he insults them.'

'He does,' said Norman, nodding. 'He says me guru's a poof, me motor-cycle's a disgrace and threatens me too. 'e's a right bastard and Rita loves him. Completely potty about him, she is. So I don't go home when he's there. And I always know when he's going to be there, coz she nicks me razors two days in advance – in preparation for his 'ighness.'

Norman buried his dirty face in his dirty hands and looked down at the wet table. It was still unwiped as the barmaid had refused the pleasure, saying she had already done it once and once was all she was going to do. I looked at my watch and it was quarter to eight and then I remembered that dinner was at seven and I was expected. Trouble. I said goodbye to the others and left.

At home, of course, I was the most popular gentleman at the table and the most popular topic was my attitude and we had a little argument over that and I lost.

In my room I was reading my book when Pook came in and sat down.

'So when are you taking Kath out?' he said. 'And when am I going to meet her?'

97

This was a shock, that he knew things about Kath. So I said, 'How did you know about her?'

And he said, 'You told me the other night – well you didn't really tell me on purpose but I overheard you panting her name in your sleep. That was in between all the kisses you were lavishing on that pillow of yours. She must be something, eh? Is she?'

I didn't know what to say, so I said, 'Lies. I don't know what you are talking about,' and turned away and found a riveting passage in Shogun – how to grow rice in a paddy field. Riveting.

'She's blond, right? And small and works in the cafeteria – I know all about her, James. But I won't tell if that's what you're worried about. Do you love her?'

'No.'

'You said you did, funny that.'

'That was only a dream. Dreams don't mean anything.'

'Sounded like a pretty good dream to me,' said Pook, smirking. I told him to shut up.

'So when are you taking her out to dinner?'

'Who said I was?'

'You did, in your sleep.'

'I don't know.'

'Have you talked to her yet?'

'Yeah, of course.'

'Liar,' he said. 'Get a bike before you take her out. Girls love motor-cycles. I don't know why but they do. They just love them. All my friends' sisters have pictures up on their walls of James Dean sitting on his motor-cycle or that man whatshisface, you know . . .'

'Brando?'

'Yeah, that's him. You *always* see him poking his nose into their rooms. Always. Listen, I could tell you a few more things about ladies and their likes, but I'm a businessman and nothing is for free, isn't that what dad said. So, what I think we should do is . . .'

'We?' said I, smelling a large rat.

'Right, "we" as in you and me; as in team; as in double trouble. We'd be perfect together, just great. Me as the brains, the man of strategy – cold, yet warm, calculating yet somehow . . . er . . . *sensitive* to the needs of a woman . . .'

'What?'

'Why there are too many to list right now; but of course for a small fee I can provide you . . .'

'Go away.'

'James, I'm serious. You know me, I'm always serious, but today I'm even more serious than on others, so what I think we should do, once you have been to the bank is . . .'

'Go away, I'm not paying for lessons on *Love. Love,*' said I, starry-eyed, 'is for free. You don't have to pay anything for that.'

'That's where you're wrong, James. That's where you are going to make your biggest mistake – and I'll tell you why. Are you sitting comfortably?'

'Get on with it.'

'Right. You see, before you and whatsherface . . .'

'Kath.'

'Right, Kath. Well before you and she can get all droopy together you are going to have to make an investment, take out a loan sort of thing, you know, so you can buy her dinner, give her presents, court her, be sweet with her, do all of that stuff before you get to sample the goodies. See what I mean?'

But before I had a chance to answer, old Pook started to run away with himself.

'. . . I'll give you an example. My friend Holcroft, now his brother has been going out with this girl for almost two months – now that's almost a lifetime, am I right?'

'Right.'

'Well he made a few fundamental errors in the beginning,

errors that me and Holcroft warned him about but he wouldn't listen because he knew better and of course now he's in a lot of trouble.'

'What trouble?'

'Well she still won't go home with him at night, and this is after two months, *unless* he puts down a *deposit* on her cab fare home in the morning. Now that's after two months of Love. What d'you think about *that*?'

Both Pook and Jack were staring at me from the other bed; then Jack started scratching.

'That's expensive.'

'Very expensive. But it could have been avoided as Holcroft and myself had told him many times, but it was just like talking to a wall – he wouldn't listen. What I suggest is that you be wise and enlist my help before it is too late.'

'For a certain fee.'

'Yeah,' said he, smiling and showing the gap in his front teeth where a big one was growing through.

'I'll think about it.'

'Good. I knew you'd see it my way. Now, we just have to work out my consultancy fee.'

'Out,' I said. He wouldn't go as he was too busy working out his fee and wondering whether or not it would be worth setting up a limited company to handle the proceeds of his endeavours. I threw him out.

15

On Thursday I went and bought a set of leathers from a motor-cycle shop in the West End and I went with Chopper, and this was in the lunch lull. The shop was full of head-banging glue sniffers and the man who helped me choose a suit was some kind of pervert who wanted me to touch the leather all the time. 'It's strong,' he'd say, 'very strong.' Then he'd rub the leather back and forth really quickly as if he was washing it and then he'd pull it and the leather would go, *p'tang!* Then he'd ask me to touch it and he'd say, 'What's it feel like?' and I'd say, 'Leather?' and he'd laugh and slap me on the shoulder and his laugh was like the mating call of a walrus. Then he'd show me more suits, some with fringed leather, some that were in two pieces, some that were black, some of different colours and all of them gave him much pleasure to test.

P'tang, p'tang! went the trousers as we walked up and down the racks of very strong smelling leather suits and all the time Chopper was saying not to bother with a two-piece but to get a one-piece. Eventually, after many p'tangs we found this plain black pretty racy number that was a one-piece. It zipped up the front and fastened around the collar with a popper. It had pads, too, on the knees and elbows, and these you could slip in and out of position by a zip. I went and tried one on. When I walked back out of the changing room the suit made so many squeaks that all the people in the shop turned my way and I had to stop walking and start smiling. They turned back and I walked over.

'What's it feel like?' the old pervert asked.

'It feels a little peculiar.'

'It's nice, isn't it?'

'Um . . . it's too small, I think.'

'Too small?' he cried. 'Certainly not. I should say it needs to be another size down . . .' He looked at me. 'Maybe two.'

One size down and I wouldn't be able to breathe.

'No, I don't think so. I'll try one up, what do you think, Chopper?'

'Two,' said Chopper.

Two sizes up and it felt like a good fit. So I bought it. Afterwards we rode back to my house, but I didn't think it would be a great idea to bring Chopper inside if Mumma was there. He waited outside, on the bike, and when I had checked to see that there was no one he came in.

He was pretty impressed with the place, saying it looked like a 'bleedin' palace' and how you could fit four of his council flats into the size of ours. I showed him all around and he was quite taken with all the richness, lifting things up, inspecting them and asking how much they were worth. He met Jack and Jack loved him. The dog followed Chopper right round the house, sniffing him. In my room I changed whilst Chopper rolled himself a joint to smoke.

'What d'you think I should buy, then?' said I.

After he had lit his joint, Chopper told me that he had a brother who dealt in second-hand machines and that he was sure he would have a couple of machines that would be of interest to me. In fact, he said, right now he had got a batch of 350 Lcs that he was trying to get rid of. The price would be good and he could guarantee that the bikes would work for a long time as his brother was a genius with machines though only thirteen years of age.

'Can we go look at them?' I asked.

'We could go tonight, if ya' like.'

At three o'clock we started work and the afternoon was

dull. In the evening we stopped off for a drink at the pub and as nobody was there we left after a pint and rode up to Hackney. We came to an awful looking place, really grey and grim it was, and this is where Chopper lived. We parked the motor-cycle in the courtyard and then rode the lift to the fifteenth floor. The lift smelt rotten and the lights didn't work and the walls were covered with graffiti. This is where his brother lived, Chopper had said, and when we knocked on the door there was a terrible fight going on between his parents. His little brother answered the door and he looked like a junior version of Chopper himself.

'All right Chopper?' said the little brother who was introduced as Jake, and Chopper smiled and we went in and walked up stairs to where the noise was coming from. The house didn't look much. It was rundown and they could have done with a maid. We went through and made tea in the kitchen. Out the window you could only see other estates that were grey and tall and grim. Whilst we made tea Chopper's mum howled at his father and I was glad when we left. We went down to the courtyard and opened up one of the garages that ran the length of the building. The garage was stacked full of motor-cycles, motor-cycle parts, workbenches and tools. Against the far wall stood two Lcs, one white and the other black. We wheeled them out and Jake started them up.

'What d'you think?' said Chopper.

'They look very fine,' I replied.

'Jake, give him a helmet, let him try it.'

I took the white one out first, running up to the end of the road and back. They were plenty quick, and at six grand on the tacho, then the motor-cycle flew charging right up to the red line in no time at all. You had to hold on on a machine like that. I was shaking all over when I brought her in.

'Good?' said Chopper.

I smiled and nodded and grinned and blipped away on the throttle.

'Good,' he said and he went and got his helmet from his bike and got on the other Lc.

'Don't drop it Chopper,' said Jake, and we went, with Chopper showing how wonderful he was with a machine, pulling a wheelie right to the end of the courtyard, before dropping it down and braking to pull out in the road. We rode around Hackney for a while and bought some beer and then went back to the garage and talked. I was so excited I couldn't stop looking at the machine, and as we drank beer Jake and Chopper showed me everything about it. Two discs, two stroke, monoshock three-fifty, chain drive. It had eight thousand miles on the clock and little Jake reckoned that there was another twenty thousand miles in the barrels before a rebore. I would have bought it right there and then if I'd had the money in my pocket, what with being so excited and taken with it and everything, but as I didn't, I couldn't, but I said I would, and when I looked at my watch it was close to ten and I'd forgotten about the time completely and now it was dark. I got the peculiars over that and quickly said goodbye to Chopper and Jake and headed off home.

Damn, old mother was heaving a wobbly at me for close on an hour after I walked through the door, with me being so late and everything. I don't feel like telling you much about it, so I won't. But I should tell you that she almost jumped clean out of her skin when she saw my leathers. Her eyes popped and it took her a moment to catch her breath before she let loose a fiery tongue that singed my ears. I ate dinner and went to bed.

Friday I went to the bank and took out eight hundred pounds of my loan to pay little Jake and after work I went round and picked up my machine. When I gave him the money he told me to watch out in the wet as the power was tricky and could come on strong in a corner, if you were accelerating, and throw a man right off. He gave me the ownership papers and Chopper lent me one of his helmets and we all went off to the pub and drank beer.

Saturday was pretty slow and I lounged around the house trying to be helpful in the morning and when that didn't work I went and bought myself a Bell, that being a helmet, and then rode around for a couple of hours having a fine time. But soon I got to wish that I could share it with someone so I called up everybody that I knew from school – but all the girls were out, or were studying, or were still at school, or I wasn't allowed to talk with them.

So I rode around some more and then I got the fine idea of riding down to Brighton as I'd heard all the other riders talk about what a good road it was. It was about five in the evening and it was beautiful, with the sun still shining strong and the sky all blue and not much traffic on the road and I rode out through Streatham and Croydon and just after Purley I joined up with a gang of Angels on a run and I rode with them down the motorway. There were maybe ten of them riding hard tail Triumphs with teardrop tanks and a few were on chopped Honda seven fifty-fours with swept back bars and chromed clocks. It was a sight with the pack of us thundering down the motorway and it made me laugh watching the faces of the car drivers as we swept by. None of them would look at us but I could tell that most of the drivers were nervous and peeped at us out the corner of their eyes. When the motorway narrowed down to two lanes for the final miles into Brighton I left the Angels to work the road because their machines were slower through the turns. I got my machine running at about ninety-five for most of the way and it felt pretty good, though she would shake a little in the turns if there was some ripples in the road. It certainly made the blood run and I felt a whole lot happier when I pulled up on the sea-front, after such a good ride.

Later I went to a film as I didn't feel like going home.

The whole cinema was packed with lovey couples. Him smooching with her, or them holding hands in contented and patient silence, or her hugging him, and these things made me lonesome and I was glad to get my ticket and take my seat in the auditorium away from all of this.

I sat sunk in my seat with my knees resting upon the seat in front and next to me sat an old man who liked popcorn and chewed it thoroughly and consistently – like a cow chews grass. In front a couple sat and he had his arm around her. She didn't look so bad but she had this annoying habit and she just could not stop touching her fringe or adjusting his arm so that it didn't touch her straight blond hair. When he touched it she'd put her head forward to free her hair, then she'd shake it and then she'd play with it so that it was swept over to one side. It was pretty tiresome.

The film was good and I knew it would be as all the riders had said so at work. It was called Mad Max. It was the story of this policeman called Max who drove around in this all special car, sometime in the future, sorting out the undesirables – they being some outlaw bandit gang of motor-cycle men on big, fine-looking, heavy-duty high-bore Kawasakis and Hondas. These bandits were a troublesome lot and went round doing a lot of raping which meant that old Max would have to slip into his leathers and make all the ladies in the cinema get a little sick for him. So once he was in his leathers he'd chase them down in his speed machine, looking tough and moody and having the country reflected in his Polaroids, and he'd try and kill them with his sawn off pump gun, and this was all great entertainment to watch if you could but the couple in front would not stop. All the time he had his damned tongue down her throat – you'd think she was suffering from tonsillitis the way he was operating. He had the horn on him all right and so after an hour or so of this all-enveloping lizard like behaviour I was starting to get ragged. Then the film comes to this scene where Max's good friend – I don't remember his name but he rides a Z1 with rear sets and a full fairing – is pursuing some outlaws and is catching them, and just when all hell is about to break loose, the man in front calmly leans across and plants her one right on the kisser. I had no choice.

'*Can't you keep your tongue in your own mouth?*' I shouted.

It just popped out like that and before I knew it there was a whole lot of shushing in the cinema and everybody's turned round and looking at me. Everybody except the lizard who is still doing some exploratory work on her tonsils. I felt a little embarrassed so I sank a little in my seat. Then, they all turn away and the lizard's still working and Max's friend is lying up half-dead and bloodied on the road side after having one fireball of a crash which I missed because of the lizard. Well, the scene carries on and so did they and I watched as if nothing had happened, only I'm fidgeting and feeling mightily embarrassed. Then he, the lizard, stopped and I saw him stop though all the time I'm looking up at the screen wondering what it is that he's going to do and knowing from my belly upwards that whatever it is it will most likely be unpleasant. Maybe you should look him right in the eye, I was thinking, be bold. Maybe he would take offence on top of the offence he took already. Besides, this lizard looks like a large well-muscled lizard. I didn't look him in the eye – I didn't get a chance as the punch came in and caught me on the bridge of the nose, bringing the tears gushing down and some blood with it.

I whelped as the crazy bastard then got up from his seat and started pummelling me. He was mad all right and I was lucky to get away with just a few other knocks on the head as he started screaming at me for being a peeping tom. If I hadn't been caught a little unawares I might have stuck around and shown him a thing or two. (I was the under nine house boxing champion) but as I was caught unawares I scarpered, with haste.

I rode home in the dark and the cool air relieved a little of the pain. When I got home it was before twelve and I was standing on the pavement looking in through the window at the parents and their friends drinking and laughing and I was hearing old José Feliciano twang his guitar. They all looked plastered and some of the very drunk ones danced. I felt all very sorry for myself knowing that I couldn't go through the front door with my face the way it was, and the thought of the climb around the building, and being tired, made me sort of miserable. I wished I had a Sherry or a Marie to come home to; even old Joan would have done.

16

All of Sunday I spent trying to avoid the parents as they had not yet found out that a motor-cycle had been purchased, though I think they suspected. It rained that day and I went to the park to feed the ducks and to think things through. I was lonesome though I tried saying to myself I wasn't but it didn't work so I knew I was. I couldn't find any ducks either and I hunted everywhere for them but I suppose they had gone on holiday on account of the weather. When I got home I'd made my mind up that on Monday I was going to ask the lady Kath out. Without a doubt.

In the evening I watched the television as the parents had gone to bed early on account of the hangovers (they didn't admit this) they had acquired from the boozing of the night before. I watched this film starring Sophie Loren. It was a musical and of course it was a love story. I switched the channel. Later there was the news and the Scot from the police station was a news item. He was at Wembley, the only person that was, and he was singing, 'Scotland, Scotland, we love you Scotland!' and he was waving a banner above his head with one hand and with the other he let off an air horn. A real blaster of a horn it was, too. The police had to take him away, but before they did the reporter managed to ask him a few questions. 'Why was he there?' the reporter asked, and the Scot told him he was supporting Scotland. 'Did he not know that Scotland weren't due to play there for another six months?' He didn't get a reply to this question. The Scot could only shriek, '*Wemmbblee! Wemmbbleee! We're goin' to Wembleeee! And we're goin' to win the cup!*' Then the Scot hiccupped and was led away. I went to bed.

The next couple of days weren't much. I got wet Monday, bought a dry suit Tuesday, had an argument that night with my dad over a television programme and stomped off to bed aggravated that they have to win every damned thing you argue about – and it doesn't seem to matter much whether they have right on their side, just winning's enough. It would also be fair to say that I wasn't in the best of moods. In fact, I was in a filthy temper for most of that day. You see, it started with a close call with a juggernaut – for them bastards are properly difficult to tell what they'll do next. I should tell you about this just to warn you that when you are sitting behind some monstrous black-smoke-belching, tarpaulin covered, high walled, big wheeled thing that has the left indicator going but is moving out to the right, don't for a moment think that he's turning right or has forgotten his blinker or something; because he hasn't. But I thought he had and we were going down Baker Street and he was in front giving me a face full of that filthy smoke that was angling out of his pipe, when I saw him go right, so I thought to myself, here's my chance. So I gave it some and hared down the inside; but he wasn't going right – he was going left into the Selfridges storage lot. So when I saw him come back, sweeping across me, cutting off my road, I could do nothing more than get on the brakes as fast as I could pull and push. Well, the motor-cycle went all sideways with the rear wheel squealing and the truck coming in on me faster and faster and I had to get off the rear brake, get her straightened up, then plough on the front with all my might, and the rear, too – but not so hard that I'd lock her up. Well, I managed it all right and pulled up just shy of the rear wheel as the truck shot into the lot. And then I shook because I was mad with myself and angry that I'd almost wiped out the bike.

Lunch was also a disaster, on both days. Stanley had me working solid right through them so that I could only grab a sandwich up in Edmonton the first day, a manky cheese and chutney, and then I had a reasonable egg and chips at Mick's in Catford. So I wasn't feeling too dandy about that, not being able to see Kath and ask her out and everything. Also, Stanley had promised me a radio at the beginning of the week and he hadn't given me one, and phone boxes that worked, or didn't have people in them, or weren't for 999 calls only, were a rarity. And a man could get himself worked up into quite a sweat running around the place looking for a box to call in from and all this running about wasted time and time wasted was jobs not done, was less money. If you didn't use the boxes you had to call in from the offices where you picked up from or made a drop and a lot of time in these offices the little secretary that sits meekly behind her desk typing can suddenly turn, just like a squall, into a raging tyrant. She can make a rider feel like the lowest, dirtiest, leper type that God ever gave wind, shooting you an icy stare should you ask her any favour to do with the telephone or indeed any other facility that the office might be able to supply. And if you do ask her, and she's one of these types, then she'll lean back a little in her chair, lift her nose so that she's not looking up at you and push out the telephone, sighing something rotten. So you make your call and you thank her but she'll never do anything more than sigh. In some offices they're so cheap that they ask you for 10p, but I had a theory that this was the secretary's doing and she was pocketing it. There was no other reason for it. My dad had already told me about tax deductions and what could be charged on the business and what couldn't and I knew telephone calls could, so they had to have been doing it for that reason only. Mind you, there were some good ones and they were as kind and warm as you'd want – letting you use the telephone and smiling and offering you tea, and some even talked to you.

Well, Wednesday was better. I worked around the West End in the morning and at lunch there was a lull so I went back to the office full of expectation, but when I parked my motor-cycle and went in to the café Kath wasn't anywhere to be seen. I asked old Chopper in a roundabout sort of way where she was and he sniffed and smiled and smoked and said it was her day off so I said, 'Oh,' and went on eating. He looked at me, though, and I reckoned he knew there was something brewing up in my heart.

After lunch I went up to see Stanley about my radio. He had one for me, he said, when I walked in.

'You'll need a number,' he said.

'A number?'

'Call sign. You superstitious?'

'Yes.'

'Too bad. The only number I got be t'erteen – it belong to Wilco before he had his accident and before dat it belong to Smiffy and he also be havin' an accident. Den, let me see – who be before 'im? I know. Johnny, dat's who it was.'

'Did he crash?'

'No, he quit after a week. Le's hope you be havin' more luck, eh?'

'Yup.'

Stanley had a hell of a way of inspiring confidence in an employee. He gave me the radio, a transformer and charger and I left him talking and screaming at the lazy good-for-nothing riders that weren't being speedy enough. Oh, he also made me sign this form that stated I was a paid up employee of Rocket Despatch and told me that I should say I was G.O.B. on arrival and not, 'I have the package in my hand, no, it's in my saddlebag, where d'you want me to go to now, Stanley?' He said that was all too long and useless.

Downstairs I met Norman standing outside the toilet

and I asked him how he was and all he could say was, 'Terrible, man.'

'Why's that, Norman?' said I.

'It's Conchita.'

'What's wrong with her?'

'She went east. The holy cow ran off to live with my guru in Bethnal Green. I'm a broken man.'

I tried to console him saying the normal muck of there being plenty more ladies (of course I didn't believe this myself as I had not yet found one) but that was useless as it turned out that it was not her that Norman was worried about – it was the guru. Then the toilet opened and out drifted Frank and Rita, high as kites, their eyes glazed and smiling.

They both said all right and floated past, smiling.

Then the afternoon work came and the radio made all the difference and got me many more jobs, though sometimes it went on the blink and I'd swear at it and shake it and then it would work. I got an airport run that afternoon and then a pickup in Sunbury coming back to Kingston and when I called in empty at Kingston Stanley had a pick up for me in Walton-on-Thames and that was a cash job so I was in the money in the evening.

After work I went to the pub and she was there. Almost spilt my beer taking it to the table, I was so nervous.

I bought a round and sat down. The pub was crowded and most of the riders were there. I saw the man with the Gold Wing and the Christmas lights who has the stereo with graphic equaliser aboard. Also the CX500 rider with the beaver skin wrapped on the helmet – he was there and some others whose helmets I knew but not their faces.

Chopper was mightily content. His foot was feeling much better and he'd tested it on an Escort that morning and the foot had come up trumps. 'Didn't hurt at all,' he said to Rita, 'not even a twitch.' Then he went on to say that he thought these new Doctor Martens he had bought, the ones with the steel toecap, were the best pair he had ever owned and he'd owned many in his time. He reckoned he could kick a hole in a wall if need be.

I sat all very quiet concentrating the mind and its eye about four feet to the left of me on little Kath. I was chewing over all the different ideas I'd had of asking her out. Dinner had to be the best bet for anything like that because you get a chance to talk, unlike a cinema. Though I was properly worried that because she worked with food all day, food would be the last thing she'd want to see in the evening. Then I thought about taking her up to the park to see the ducks or to go out in a row boat but that idea might not work because of the time that we finished work and anyway she might not hold much for ducks. So dinner was what it should be.

I was just working up the courage to start talking to her when she gets up and says that she has to go home. I thought I'd missed my chance but luckily old Chopper suddenly remembers – and he remembers this looking my way – that he had arranged to take Sherry out. So there was poor stranded Kath without a ride home. I gulped down a large swig of beer for courage and said, 'I can take you home if you want.'

Chopper grinned and Frank lifted an eyebrow and Kath said, 'Can you?'

'Yes,' said I. 'I'm going home that way.'

'I thought you lived in Knightsbridge,' said Rita.

'I do.'

'Hackney is the other side of London.'

'I know, but I . . . um . . . was going to go over there anyway. I want to go see Jake about a few things on the bike.'

''Course you were,' said Rita, smiling at Chopper. My face started going red and then Kath said that she'd like that and I was oh so happy and we left.

Outside I started to get a little worried as I hadn't taken

a pillion on this machine and I wanted to make the right impression and so when she got on I was careful about not stalling when we rode off. I didn't bother trying to impress her with my weaving. Apart from the fact that I was pretty lousy at it I liked having her so close and I wanted the journey to take as long as possible. When we stopped at the light at Farringdon Street Kath leaned forward and said she didn't want to go home.

'What would you like to do?' I said, all nervous.

'Let's go for a walk by the river,' and so we did.

The tide was out when we got there and we walked along the shore and a police boat came by and above the river some gulls worked. I threw rocks.

We had a good talk and must have covered most things and we laughed and I loosened up a bit. We talked about family and work and school and we laughed and she said she was going to be an actress and I said I hadn't a clue what the hell to do though I mentioned that I thought it wouldn't be bad being a duck.

'Why a duck?' she asked.

I told her how it was with ducks; how you can go any-where you please, how you have no responsibility; and what it is that a duck does with himself during a day. Kath thought all of this was hysterical – a big, fat, flying, feathered joke.

'It's no joke,' I said, 'I'm serious.'

'I think you're mad.'

'Crackers?'

She liked that one and laughed. We walked around a while talking some more and throwing stones and then she said she had to go home and I took her. She lived in Bethnal Green not Hackney in a smiliar block to Chop-per's. On every balcony laundry was drying. So then we said goodbye and she said goodbye and I said goodbye again and so did she and so did I and then I knew that if I didn't say it then I probably never would so I said it.

'Would you come to dinner with me, sometime?'

I was really nervous, I really was. 'I mean if you haven't got anything better to do, I'd like to buy you dinner. Would you like that?' I thought I'd never get the words out; but they came out, though they were sort of strangled sounding and I think my face was going red again as she thought about it.

'Yes,' she said.

'You would?' said I not believing what the ears told me. 'Really?'

'Yes.'

'That's great,' I said and I was smiling and grinning like I hadn't done for a long time.

'Well when could you come? Tomorrow? If you like we could go out tomorrow?'

Kath couldn't do tomorrow or the next day. In fact she was pretty booked up and wasn't going to be free for a week. I didn't ask why.

'What sort of food then?'

'You choose.'

'All right.'

We smiled and said a few more goodbyes and then she left. I got home and I had completely forgotten that I was still in my leathers and when I walked through the front door old mother was on the phone.

'Yes, of course, you know James is working now,' she was saying as I put my key in the lock. 'What does he do? Oh, he's a . . . um . . . Communications Executive. That's right. . . Proud of him did you say? Oh yes, terribly. We . . .'

I had the door open and I was standing there looking at Mother look at me. I still had my helmet on.

'James?' she said nervously. Then she backed away a bit and held the telephone as a weapon. 'Is that you?'

'It is,' I said and removed the helmet.

'What on earth are you wearing? Did your father give you that?'

'No. I bought it for my job. It's leather. You like it?'

'No.'

'I could lend it to you if you did. I hear leather is big this year.'

'Why are you late?'

'I had a flat.'

'You had one yesterday.'

'That was the back. This time it's the front, sorry.'

I went through to my room to change and before I did I stood in front of my mirror and worked out the best position for my radio. I slung it like a gun from hip on a belt. The Wild West, the grey frontier, no, the Wet Frontier, scalps, my trusty steed, savages – these things I was thinking about when Pook popped his head round the door and shot me in the back with his fingers.

Bang! B'bang!

'What d'you want?' I asked.

He wanted to know everything, starting with the articulated lorries and ending with Kath. I told him as I fixed up the radio and transformer and charge unit and he wouldn't stop fiddling with them.

'Where you going to take her?'

'I don't know – maybe San Simeons.'

'She'll hate it. The food's terrible. Take her to McDonalds. There you get good decent food. I take Jack there sometimes. He loves it.'

'Kath isn't a dog.'

'Oh. Is she pretty?'

'Of course.'

'You say that about every girl you take out.'

'I know, but this is the truth.'

'When can I meet her?'

'You can't.'

'Why not? Then I could tell you whether she's worth the effort.'

'Don't ask me.'

'Okay. I'll ask you something else. Does she have big knockers?'

Just at that moment Mother starts howling, 'Jayyames?'

'Hark!' said Pook. 'Here comes Silver, the Lone Ranger's trusty nag.'

'Very funny, get out.'

Pook left, Mum entered, we had a great little argument and I went to bed.

17

Stanley paid me a hundred and thirty pounds for the week's work. That wasn't as good as some of the boys, but it wasn't bad for my first week in the saddle, all things considered. On Thursday and Friday, it was cold with showers. All day long the roads were damp and they were no fun to ride on. Stanley had me working out in Middlesex most of Thursday and on Friday I had a long run through the lunch hour, so I never got back to the cafe. When the weekend came I was tired and did a lot of sleeping and thinking about the dinner. I had got nervous about this dinner. My heart would quicken and my paws would start sweating just thinking about it. I got in an awful mess working out the best place to take her – that was after working out the best type of food to feed her. In the end I reasoned that Italian was the safest choice. All the other places are a little dodgy – like Chinese, it is good food but if you have a tummy that's not dandy, a person can be put off by all those poor dead ducks, plucked and hanging in the window with a hook through their heads. Then there was a story old Lucy told me, a horror story, of a friend of hers (another horror story) who had eaten in a French place and had almost ruptured something inside of her because of some bones that weren't even supposed to be in the dish, but were. And Indian: you've got to have the mouth of a fire eater to cope with that stuff. So, it had to be Italian. (English wasn't worth considering.)

After a load of phone calls enquiring about table size, guitar players, candle-lit dinners and all that other romantic mood making material, I picked out this little beauty of a place in Fulham. It had everything, the works, right down to Sale Pepe, the resident Flamenco guitarist. I was really excited about this little place but when I rang up Kath to tell her, she said it was no good as it was too far away. So I had to find somewhere else and found this little place in Greek Street. Then I waited for Wednesday. It took a long time arriving.

And finally I was getting ready in my room. I was panicking as I didn't know and hadn't thought about what to wear. Pook was watching me, throwing a ball up against the wall.

'What d'you think of this?' said I holding up one of my finest most uncomfortable shirts that came all the way from the men's department at Harrods.

'Not much,' Pook said.

'What's wrong with it?'

'It's a little dated, James. You want to wear something a little more . . . you know what I mean?'

'No.'

'Well, you want something that *she* likes. If she's a punk you be a punk. If she likes all that skinhead stuff go buy yourself a pair of boots and one of them jackets they wear. You have to make yourself appealing, you see.'

'I don't.'

I stood in front of the mirror. What a fine sight, me and my grey flannels and my striped shirt.

'What d'you think, then?'

'It's all right.'

'Is that all you can say?'

'That's all it is.'

'All right, why don't you go get me a little of that cologne from the parents' bathroom – the final touch. Please. Well?'

'You get it.'

'If I get it they'll see me and old Mother will want to know everything. Help me.'

'I might.'

120

Well, when Pook says 'I might' he means he will – if I pay him. That's how it is with him now. Everything is business. It wasn't always that way – he used to fetch things when he was small on a please only. Unfortunately Dad wised him up.

'How much, then?'

'You got any pens?'

'No.'

'All right. I'll get the cologne if you walk the dog in the morning.'

'Sure.'

So he went off and returned a few minutes later with the cologne. He gave it to me and said, 'Does it work?'

'What d'you mean?' said I slapping some around the neck area.

'That lotion. Does it work with the girls?'

'I don't know what you are talking about.'

'I mean do they get sexy with you when you wear it?'

'I don't know.'

'They do in adverts, always. They go sick. That's why Dad wears it. He's got two bottles of the stuff. I bet you didn't know that did you? He hides the good stuff behind the laundry basket because he knows you take it. He thinks I don't know about it; but I do and it smells great. It's bound to be irresistible.'

The little bugger.

'All right, how much?'

'I'll be fair with you James . . .'

'Don't be fair. How much?'

'Your record deck for a week.'

'Deal.'

I waited for him to get up and go get it; but he didn't go. So I said, 'Go get it.'

Pook smiled and dug around in his pockets.

'Here,' he said, pulling out a small, crystal bottle with a gold label. 'She'll love it.'

18

It was dusk when I rode up to Soho. I parked in Moor Street, where there are a lot of Despatch Riders in the daytime. I was twenty-five minutes early, being so terrified of being late and of missing her. The restaurant was in Greek Street, I made sure of that. I walked past it.

I walked down Old Compton Street, past the arcades and half expected to see Chopper, but I didn't. I walked up Frith Street past the restaurants and smelt the food cooking inside and saw couples going in and out and it didn't make me jealous at all. I arrived at the restaurant at ten to eight.

There was a mustachioed, fat-on-pasta man at the front desk. I told him I had a table booked for two in the name of Montgommery.

'Ah, yes.' he said as he fingered in the bookings book. 'Montgommery. This way please.'

The fatman walked me to a table right by the kitchen and sat me down.

'Has a girl come in here with electric white hair?' I asked.

'No, I don't think so,' the fatman said, and handed me a menu.' The Specials today, are –'

'Would you wait until she arrives until you tell me?'

'Sorry. Would you like a drink?'

'Beer, please.'

He went away through the swing doors, to the kitchen. The restaurant was empty. A few waiters were standing by the window facing the street, talking. All the tables had white cloths. A couple came in and the fatman brought me my beer. It was now ten past eight.

Eight thirty. She had not arrived. I had drunk two beers. I went through all the possibilities: train strike (unlikely); she had lost the address (I gave it to her twice); they had an argument at home and Vera banned her from going out . . .

'More beer, sir?' said the waiter from behind my shoulder.

'No. Are you sure a girl with electric white hair hasn't come in?'

'No, I tell you no, ees no, okay?'

'All right. Give me another beer.'

'Okay.'

The restaurant, I had decided, was a dump. It had all the right elements. This was a dump and all the clients were the flies that came to feed at the dump. A little big for flies but they had similar manners, I watched them. There was this enormous couple that sat at the table where the waiters had been talking earlier. They were extraordinarily fat for humans.

'More beer?'

'Yes, another, please.'

They sat at their table opposite one another and ate with their mouths open, and talked with their mouths full. How do flies eat? I think they also eat with open mouths.

'More beer?'

'Why not, ol' fatman.'

'What?'

'Nothing.'

In fact I'm sure they eat with open mouths. They've got no mothers to teach them manners. And their girlfriends probably eat exactly the same. Those two, over there, are identical in every way, except she's got big, bustin' out boobies, and he hasn't. That isn't strictly true. He's got a pretty enormous chest on him too, but it's not as big as hers. She's bigger than Chesty Morgan. I'll bet she's even bigger than ol' Lucy, I was thinking.

'More beer?'

'What time is it?'

'Nine o'clock.'

'You sure you haven't seen a girl . . .?'

'No! I tell you no beeefore, and I tell you no, again. Okay?'

'All right. Give me another beer and then give me the bill and I'll go.'

'Okay.'

'Listen, come here.'

'What?'

'I got some advice for you.'

'What?' said fatman.

'Buy some insect repellent. It'd work wonders in here.'

'What?'

'Nothing. More beer.'

Later, I was walking around the place trying to find my bike. I couldn't see it anywhere. I walked up all these streets and then down others, but the damned motor-cycle had disappeared. I called out to these two ladies standing on a street corner.

'Ladies, ladies, ladies. Have you seen a motor-cycle parked near here?'

One of them was white and the other was black, both pig ugly. I think I was a bit drunk.

'What you say, boy?' said the black one.

'I lost my motor-cycle. Have you seen it?'

'No,' said the black one.

'I'm Ahoor,' the white one says, and I notice she speaks with an Irish accent.

'Ahoor, nice to meet you. My name is James.'

I held out my hand.

'I don't want to shake yer han', boy.'

'I thought you were introducing yourself.'

125

'I was, I'm Ahoor.'

'I know that you said that, and I said my name's James. Nice to meet you Ahoor.'

'No. I am a hoor.'

'Ahoor?'

'A hooor.'

'A hoor?'

'Yes, a hooor.'

'A whore?'

They both smiled.

'You two are whores?'

'Ay, you're a smart boy, aren't you?'

'Really? You mean, like a prostitute?'

'You're a fine lookin' maan. You mosst hahve some money to play with?'

'I've never met a prostitute before. Say, what's it like?'

'If you got some money, we can show you.'

'Can't you just tell me about it?'

'He's no good, Mary,' said the black woman.

'He might have something. You want to feel my tits?'

'No, I think I'd better go now, I'm flat broke.'

'You must want something?' said Ahoor.

'No, I think I'd better go. Are you sure you haven't seen my motor-cycle?'

They turned and walked away, I turned and tried walking away, but fell on the floor. I got up and when I was walking I still could not find the motor-cycle. It was too dark. I came to a bench, sat down, and fell asleep.

I was asleep for some time and when I woke, the night had turned cold. My head was a little clearer. I sat up. There was a small, hunched and ragged figure sitting at the end of the bench. He had a beard that fell to his chest. He was bent over so that his elbows rested on his knees; his head swivelled on his shoulders as he watched the pedestrians come to and fro. The bench was very uncomfortable and my back ached. I was opposite a theatre in Wardour

Street, and behind me was the park.

'Who are you?' I asked.

'Meee?' he screeched. I noticed he held a can of Special Brew. 'Mick's the name. Who are you?'

'My name is James, pleased to meet you.'

'I bet you aren't.'

'I am pleased. How long have you been sitting here?'

'OOooohhh!' Mick said wailing. His voice was high, and his bearded face contorted. 'Fifty years. Maybe more, maybe less. I don't rightly know.'

'D'you know how long I've been sleeping here?'

'Nope.'

'D'you know how long you've been sitting here?'

'Nope.'

Mick was watching a young lady as she walked towards us from Shaftesbury Avenue. He started growling. The lady wore metal heeled shoes that sang out with each step. Mick raised himself slowly from the bench, and shouted at her, when she was only fifteen yards away, *'Change yer underwear!'*

The lady turned, and walked away in the opposite direction. Mick sat down.

'Why did you say that?'

'Why? Why? *Why?* What's why? 'ere,' Mick whispered and gestured with his finger that I should move closer, as if he had some enormous secret to tell me. I leaned across the bench and he shouted at me.

'Change yer underwear!!' he bellowed.

I didn't wait for him to finish. I threw up. 'You filthy bugger,' shouted Mick.

I got up and I ran like a bastard all the way down Old Compton Street and halfway down. I remembered where the old bike was parked. I reached the motor-cycle, unhitched the helmet and my hands were shaking. What a madman that tramp was! A complete lunatic. I fumbled in my pocket for the keys, started the motor-cycle, and rode home slowly, not wishing to be stopped and breathalysed.

At home I still couldn't stop thinking about that tramp. As I was climbing over the roof, I wondered what would happen if someone did do just what he asked, right in front of him: changed their underwear. It would probably encourage him, I thought. Coming down the drainpipe I could see the light behind the curtains in the parents' bedroom and I wondered if they knew I was out. I hoped not. I jumped down from the boiler roof, in the darkness, to the garage roof, walked across the garage roof to my window, opened the window and climbed in.

'James?'

It was Pook.

'Yup.'

'Where have you been? Did you stay at her house?'

He was lying in the other bed. Jack was there also.

'What time is it?'

He looked at his watch. It was one of those types that had every possible function a watch could have.

'Three ten.'

I must have slept for hours, on that bench.

'She didn't turn up.'

'She didn't?'

'No.'

'So what have you been doing?'

'I'll tell you tomorrow. Did the parents check to see if I was in?'

'No.'

'Good.'

'Good-night, James.'

'Good-night.'

Pook woke me early in the morning. He brought me a cup of tea. I had a terrible hangover.

'What's the matter?' Pook said.

'My head.'

'Did you get drunk?'

128

'Yes.'

'And she didn't turn up?'

'No.'

'What are you going to do?'

'I don't know.'

'D'you think she did it on purpose?'

'I don't know. Did you put any sugar in this?'

'Three.'

'What are you doing?'

'I'm taking the record deck, like you said I could.'

'Did you walk the dog?'

'Yup. I knew you couldn't. You really were plastered last night.'

'What time is it?'

'Half eight.'

Pook opened the curtains and the light seared the brain. My clothes were all over the floor.

'Breakfast's ready! C'mon, boys! 'my mother shouted from down the hall.

'I don't think I can eat breakfast. Will you tell her I don't feel too well?'

'Are you going to work?'

'Yes.'

Pook and Jack went out of the room. I laid in my bed and felt sick, and thinking of Kath made me feel more sick. After a while I got up. I went to the bathroom and drank water from the tap, with two Paracetemol. Then I dressed. My head hurt.

'Bye Mum,' I said as I walked out the house.

'Don't be late for dinner this evening, darling.'

'Right.'

It was about ten to nine, and the sun was shining and there was a lot of traffic on Sloane Street. A 137 came along and all the people waiting at the stop boarded the bus. The bus pulled away. I called Stanley on the radio.

'One three,' I said.

There was no reply and there were no other voices talking on the circuit. He had not yet arrived at the office. Pook came out of the building, waved to my mother – who stood in the window – , and fooled her, by walking along the pavement until she was unable to see him, then doubling back, close to the wall of the building next to ours.

'James,' he said, 'I had a thought.'

'What?'

'Get a hair cut.'

'That's your thought?'

'Seriously. Get your hair cut short, like Chopper's.'

'Why?'

'Didn't you say how she loved short hair? Huh, didn't you?'

'So?'

'So, if you get your haircut, you'll be irresistible.'

'I'm not going to see her again.'

'Why not?'

'She stood me up. I'd be too embarrassed.'

'You're wet. You really are. That's pathetic.'

'I can't help it. I'm upset.'

'Are you going to give up before you've started?'

'Yes.'

'You're sad, James.'

'I feel it.'

'Listen, you just have to resign yourself to the fact that she's going to be a difficult one to catch. Treat it as a challenge. Some girls love to play hard to get. They like being chased. It makes them feel good.'

'What are you trying to say?'

'Well, if she's so wonderful, as you've told me she is many times, why give up over a minor setback?'

'What about my pride?'

'Stuff that. Who knows, she might have a good excuse for not turning up.'

'I doubt it.'

'Anyway, I've got to go to school. Think about it.'

During the morning session, I rode around thinking about it. Stanley kept me occupied with west ones. I picked them up in west one, and I dropped them in west one. It is the worst place to work. So much for that nonsense of his about Rocket being a distance firm. I spent more time walking up and down the lousy stairs to the offices of the cheap clients than I did on the motor-cycle. With the sun out, and wearing leathers, I was roasted. At one o'clock, I went back to the office. I bought a cheese and tomato roll from a sandwich bar on the Strand, and parked the bike opposite, but out of sight of, Vera's.

Some other riders were parked down the street and they were talking. One of them read a motor-cycle paper. I lay supine on the motor-cycle with my feet hitched over the handlebars, in the sun, and listened to all the radios on the bikes amplify Stanley's conversation with three-three. There was some problem with the job. My head was still painful.

'Hey, Jimbo!' It was Chopper. He was leaving the pub. 'I hear she stood you up.'

'That's right.'

'She said to me some cousin of hers turned up. All the way from Italy.'

'Is that so?'

'That's what she says.'

'Did she say anything else?'

'She says she tried calling you, but got a wrong number.'

'She did?'

'That's what she said. Haven't you talked to her yet?'

'No.'

'Why not?'

'I'm a little embarrassed.'

'Don't worry about that.'

'Where did you get your haircut?'

'Why?' he said, and he spat.

'I need a haircut. Look at this stuff. It gets in my eyes. Difficult to see with. It is.'

I showed Chopper how it is when my hair wasn't swept back. It all hung in front of my eyes.

'You see, it's no good, it'll kill me.'

He laughed and said, 'If you want a haircut come down to Andy's in the All Saints, he'll sort you out proper.'

We rode across London and I thought that this was very stupid, going off and getting a haircut to please a girl: A girl who was not so keen. Old Mother would go through the roof. There was no doubt about it.

Chopper could ride much faster than I could in the traffic. He was very good at weaving around the moving cars, vans, lorries, buses and taxis. I was terrible at it. I went along a line of stationary cars, waiting at a traffic light on the Edgware Road, knocking each wing mirror of each car on either side of me out of position. I had all the drivers leaning out the car windows, swearing at me. It was quite an achievement.

We rode through Paddington and Bayswater and turned off Westbourne Grove, to head north on a narrow side-street that skirted a large, grey council estate. Soon, we were in the All Saints.

'You want Hash, man?' said this tall, gangly, big-lipped, black gentleman as he slid to a halt on his wheels. ''Coz if you want it, man, I got it. Good Hash, man. Real wicked stuff. Now if you want smoke Bush, I got Bush. Wicked Bush. Check it, man.'

So this black pulls out a matchbox, opens it and Chopper tells him we don't want anything.

'Cha!' said the black as a gang of other blacks come charging down the street towards where we're parked yelling out what they have to sell.

'..Bush, 'ere.'

'White boy want smoke Hash, me got Hash.'

'I got the best Sensi in the street, you buy from me man.

If it no good you come find me. You can trust Winston.'

'Decent deal 'ere, decent deal 'ere!'

And so on.

''uck off 'unts,' said Chopper. 'We don't want nothing.'

'That's right,' said I. 'I'm here for a haircut.'

''aircut? What you do that for, boy. Nobody want see yer ugly mug. Wooman much prefer dope smokin' to hair cuttin'. You Raas!'

We left them and went into a small barbers shop called Andy's. The blacks ran off like dogs down the street.

Andy was small, dark, Greek and fat. He was also white, an unexpected sight in this part of London. As legend goes, Andy arrived in London in the immigrant boom of the mid-fifties, with enough Drachmas in his pocket to start up a small business. In Greece, Andy had trained for many years as a hair dresser, and on arrival in London, he decided, naturally enough, that he should try and pursue a career in hair. But he had no relations on these shores and no real idea of where to look for a suitable location for his business. He had only his faith to guide him. (He was a stout member of the Greek Orthodox Church.) He reasoned that he wanted to buy in an area where he could trade with fellow immigrants. He knew he could not possibly compete with the top salons for business, not yet. He visited a crooked Real Estate Agency, mentioned that he wanted to buy in an immigrant area, was shown a book of properties for sale and spotted, almost immediately, a property in a street that had been completely rebuilt, and was, according to the realtor, 'An area bursting with immigrants'.

'What is the name of this street?' asked Andy in his pidgin English.

'It is called the All Saints Road.'

After a quick consultation in the Hugo's pocket dictionary, the English was translated to Greek, and the Greek, to a Greek, was an omen.

'How much?' asked Andy.

The Real Estate Agent quoted him a price of four hundred pounds, but also added that he thought it would be no good for Andy, because there was a gentleman coming in that same afternoon who was, more likely than not, going to buy it. It was unfortunate for Andy that he was naive and ignorant in the mores of business practice. He panicked.

'You don't have any more shop properties in immigrant areas?'

'No, that's it. They're selling like hot cakes.'

Andy bought the property that afternoon. He had not visited it. He has been there ever since, cursing his bad luck to be in a neighbourhood where it is against the religion of the Rastafarian people to have their hair cut. Now, as compensation for the lack of customers, he will only cut hair short. It is said that he only does this in order to keep his hand in at the art of hair cutting. He refuses to do trims. When we walked in, the first thing I noticed was the smell of incense.

'Andy,' said Chopper. 'This is James.'

Andy was stropping his cut-throat back and forth on a piece of brown leather. He stood behind the barber's chair, where a young lad with a greased quiff sat, waiting to have his neck shaved. Andy was wearing his apron. He grunted, and started work.

'Sit down,' said Chopper.

There was a green plastic and vinyl couch against the wall. On the wall was a cross. I sat underneath the cross. Not knowing the history of the street, and never having seen dope dealers before, made me ask all sorts of stupid questions. Chopper looked a little pained and answered some, and didn't answer others. The blue-jean man with the quiff, got up, paid Andy, looked at himself in the mirror, like a vain bastard would, and left the shop.

'You,' Andy said. 'Whadda' you want?'

'A trim, please.'

'No trims. You get short or very short, like him.'

With the cut-throat, Andy gestured at a picture of Yul Brynner from that old Western, *The Magnificent Seven*.

'Nice and clean, whadda' you say?'

'That's good,' Chopper said.

'Very nice,' I said. 'But I don't mind washing my hair. I think I'll just have it short.'

A lot of my hair went with the clippers as they worked one side, and around to the back, and around to the other side, until all of that was short. Now, the only long hair was on top. He cut that hair with scissors and then all was short.

My whole face changed. Andy was showing me myself, in the hand mirror. Everything looks larger now, I thought. Your mouth, your nose, your eyes, your forehead. Your nose. Your nose, look at it. It's enormous, it fills your whole face. Boy, you are ugly now.

'Whadda' you think?' said Andy.

'I think I'm in trouble.'

'You'll get used to it,' Chopper said.

On the motor-cycles we sat and strapped on our helmets. The blacks didn't bother us, and we rode away.

That evening, I felt so depressed about the gargantuan size of my nose, I went home after work, and stayed in my room. I didn't eat supper, I couldn't sleep, it was dark, and I went up on the roof.

I sat up there for a few hours, sitting on a ledge, with the wind and the traffic below. I thought grim things. What were they going to think? Marie, she hates short hair. Mother, she's the same. Kath, she's going to think you're the ugly duckling. It was almost worth crying about.

19

In the morning, I was feeling a little better. My haircut had not been given a public viewing at home. Pook was out with a friend the night before, so were the parents. I was up and dressed before the house was awake. I made some breakfast and gobbled Vitamin E in the hope that it would stimulate some activity with the old follicles. Today, I was going to confront Kath, certainly I was.

By lunch, I estimated that I had earned over thirty-five pounds, a good amount of money to earn even for the top riders in the company. I started with a couple of jobs going south of the river, a double up, dropping first in Wimbledon and then onto Kingston. When I called in empty at Kingston, I struck gold. Old Stanley had a pick up in Basingstoke, coming back to the West End. At Basingstoke, I called in G.O.B. and he had another pick up, this time from the airport. When I had dropped the Basingstoke and the airport in the West End, it was just after one. I had twelve pounds in my pocket from the Kingston job, which was cash. I was hungry and pleased and went to the cafeteria.

I couldn't see Kath when I walked in. I ordered some food from Vera, and sat at a table. As the day was warm, most of the riders sat outside on their motor-cycles eating their food. There was nobody inside that I knew. Then old Norman walked in, looking dirtier than ever, and grinning.

'All right?' said Norman.

'Fine,' I said. 'In fact, very good.'

Norman sat at the table and started to complain. He complained and moaned about everything that he knew about, and when he had exhausted those subjects he turned the conversation – which wasn't a conversation but was more like a party political broadcast – to the subjects he knew nothing about. He told me his views on politics. He said there weren't enough dope smokers in Parliament.

'Is that what's wrong with this government?'

'Yup.'

'Fine.'

Then, he talked of the police, Frank, and the Sus Laws. In his opinion they were all connected. Frank was a police plant in the squat, of this he was convinced, and soon he was to be arrested.

'It's all right. I've made provisions,' Norman said.

'Provisions for what?'

'For Hercules, Agamemnon, Odysseus and Athena. I killed them.'

'You did, Norman?' I said, thinking the man had flipped.

'Yes, I had to. Look.'

Norman started to unzip his fly.

'I don't want to look, Norman. I've got one of my own.'

There was no stopping him. My God, I thought, the toilets must be blocked. Fortunately, something plastic appeared.

'D'you wear nappies, Norman?'

'No.'

There was a lot of activity going on, one last effort, and then a sigh of relief.

'Come here.' Norman said, beckoning to me to join him under the table. He looked about the cafeteria to make sure nobody was watching. Everybody was.

'What is it?' I said crouched over under the table.

'Shhh!' he whispered. 'Not so loud, they can hear you. They have spies everywhere.'

'Who, Norman?'

'I can't tell you. They might be listening.'

'All right. What's in the bag?'

'Hercules, Agamemnon, Odysseus and Athena.'

'Oh yes, d'you have their ashes in there?'

The bag looked like it was full of ashes. I didn't know what in the hell he was talking about. I thought it best to humour him.

'No, their leaves.'

'Their leaves?'

'Yes, I chopped them up this morning.'

'I thought they died a long time ago.'

'No. I killed them this morning, before Frank was awake.'

'Norman, they were ancient Greeks and one was a goddess. Goddesses and ancient Greeks didn't live in the squat.'

'Yes they did, they lived in my bedroom.'

'In your bedroom?'

'That's right, they lived behind the curtain.'

'What did they do behind the curtain, Norman?'

'They grew.'

'Into what?'

'Into healthy grass plants.'

'Oh, I see,' I said. 'And now that they are dead, what will you do with them, cremate them?'

'That's right. Got to smoke the lot.'

'But the bag is very big, Norman.'

'Jack,' Norman corrected.

'Sorry. Jack,' I said.

'That's all right, I'll just roll 'em larger.'

'What about work? Can you ride a motor-cycle when you're high on this stuff?'

'I do it all the time.'

The food was slapped down on top of the table. I wriggled up onto the bench leaving Norman hiding underneath.

'Nice haircut, James. It suits you,' Kath said, as she walked off to collect some more plates from the other tables. It is a funny thing, but a comment like that can make a lad go all soft inside. All that sorry feeling I had felt over the past few days had turned bad and gone angry. Now I felt just like I felt before and that was all wanting her. I ate my lunch and Norman was still waiting for his when Kath came to clear the table.

'Can I talk to you please, Kath?' I asked feeling nervous now.

'Go ahead.'

'In private.'

We went outside. She looked beautiful, she really did. She wore these jeans that stopped halfway down her gorgeous calves. And had on this top thing that was red and big and all form-fitting.

'What d'you want?' she said.

'What . . . um . . . happened?' I said all very shyly.

'When?' she said, and turned her lovely big-brown-eyed small-featured head, in profile, to look at the reflection in the glass front. 'How do I look, James?'

'You look gorgeous.'

'I feel like a tramp, look at these clothes.'

She did not have to ask to make me look; the old eyes hadn't stopped looking.

'They look great on you.'

'They don't. They're old and out of fashion. How's a girl meant to go to proper auditions in clothes like these?'

'When do you go to auditions?'

'All the time. Now, what did you want?'

She stopped looking at herself and looked at me. I looked away. How big were her breasts, I wondered.

'What I wanted to know was, um, why, um, didn't you

come, um, to dinner on Wednesday night. You didn't turn up and I was not sure why, that's all.'

'Didn't I tell you?'

'Nope.'

'I thought I had.'

'You hadn't.'

'My cousin arrived from Italy. She's just like Sophie Loren was when she was her age, such a beautiful girl, makes me all jealous.'

'You shouldn't be.'

'Are you flattering me, James?'

'No, it's the truth.'

She giggled. 'Well anyway, I hadn't expected her for another month and she turning up as she did, well, I couldn't leave her, could I?'

'I suppose you couldn't. You could have called to say you couldn't make it. I waited for you in this lousy restaurant for over an hour. Damn waiter kept giving me too much beer. Made me all drunk.'

'I didn't have your number. I would have called otherwise.' She turned to look at herself again.

'I gave it to you and you wrote it down on the back of your order pad.'

'I didn't.'

'Take a look and see.'

It was written on the pad, right at the bottom. Old Kath pretended not to see it. She was a great pretender. Finally she sees the number.

'Is this it?' she said all innocently, putting on this face that was supposed to make me feel guilty for making her guilty.

'You know something, you're going to be a great actress, you really are. You've got natural ability. Going to be a star, absolutely you are. No doubt about it. You're a definite natural.'

'D'you think I lied to you?'

Yes, certainly I did. Sure of it, I was. There could not have been any doubt about it. But I got nervous. I hate arguing. I really hate it.

'No, I don't think you lied,' I said.

'Good. So let's try again.'

'You want to try again?'

'Yes.'

'When?'

'Whenever,' she said and she was doing her lipstick in profile showing enormous white teeth. My God look at those breasts. Turn away, boy, or be smitten forever. What was it Confucius said about being burnt twice?

'How 'bout the weekend?' I said.

'No, no good. My cousin's here. I've got to look after her.'

'Of course. Maybe early next week?'

'Yes, I'd like that. No. No.'

'No?'

'No, I can't, I forgot. I won't be allowed to leave her alone.'

'All right. Why don't you let me know when you can? And if you don't want to go out for dinner maybe we could go shopping.'

'I'll call you.'

'Good.'

When I was alone, I was thinking and smiling. The clouds had come across in the sky and a few motor-cycles were in the street. I walked back to my motor-cycle parked next to Stanley's clamp-proof car. The car had three-quarter inch steel plates welded to each wheel well. Well, she has your number now. Now, there will be no excuses. The last time was an accident. It couldn't be helped, you know that. There was a cry from down the street as I was riding away. It was Norman.

'They're here!' he shouted, running at full pelt, wrestling with his zip.

'Who?' I shouted as he tore past.

'The Drug Squad,' he shouted back.

Suddenly the street came alive. Riders came running out of the Rocket building like fighter pilots under orders to 'scramble'. Motor-cycle engines spluttered into life, were stomped into gear and thundered away down the street. In the wing mirror, I watched Norman running down the street with his stubborn Suzuki. He jumped aboard, let out the clutch and the motor-cycle threw him off.

The transit van rumbled slowly along the street and halted by Stanley's car. The street was empty. The rear doors of the van opened slowly. Two traffic wardens, both wearing spectacles, armed with ticket pads, climbed down the rear steps and had a small very important conference whilst circling Stanley's car. A lot of head shaking and scratching of chins and kicking of clamp plates could be seen in my mirror. They were deeply disturbed that Stanley had parked his car, against their wishes, on a double yellow. He refused to take his car to the meter section of the street and had argued with them on many occasions in the past.

'Before I had dis, right?' he said to me when I was waiting for work in the riders room one afternoon the previous week, 'they fockin' come an' ticket me, den dey clomp me, right? Den, dey charge me good, rightfully earnt money to fockin' get back what I an' I own already. Cha, they vex me, man. It's not honest and not right, and I ain't payin' nottin' for de privilege. I work 'ere, it's my money in dat buildin', and it's my *right* to park outside. Fock 'em.'

Stanley was given a standing ovation by the riders present and, as appreciation for his sentiments, the traffic wardens sent him a 'Get Well Soon' card attached to a court summons to appear before a magistrate two days ago. Stanley thought it unwise to go to court, hired a lawyer, was fined, paid the fine and thought it was all over. Today, the traffic wardens were out to get their revenge. I watched as the tall warden with a hunched back looked nervously about the street before talking, in very distracted tones, into his radio handset. My eye caught a fleeting glimpse of a figure on the roof of the Rocket building. The warden finished his conversation, put the headset back on his lapel and started to rub his hands together.

Why was he looking so pleased with himself? I wondered. There was some joke that the pair of them thought magnificent. They were both laughing and fingering their ticket pads when the first of the eggs exploded on the pavement, sending the pair of wardens running for cover.

'Ark! Ark! Ark! Ark!' squeaked the figure from the top of the roof as the second egg overshot its target. The third didn't and thudded on to the top of the roof spilling its mucous contents in a magnificent floral pattern that stretched the length of the roof and began to drip and dribble a path earthwards bisecting the rear windscreen in two.

'Ark! Ark! Ark! Ark!' cried the leather clad figure, who bore a striking resemblance to old Frank, standing on the roof's parapet. 'Breakfast's ready!' he shouted. 'Come and get it!'

The next three delicately thrown lobs were dedicated to the reorganisation of colour on the good wardens' suits. The eggs splashed, splattered and dropped, near, above, and on the two cowering wardens who crouched, not very successfully, behind a builders' van.

'Ark! Ark! Ark! Ark!'

The wardens were running across the street to the open doors of the transit van when I spotted the lumbering bulk of a long, slow-moving, flat-bedded, tall, steel-craned, police recovery truck, entering the street. That is why they were laughing, I thought. Now, on the roof, there was nobody to be seen. The birdman had flown. There could only be one reason why this recovery truck had chosen to come down this street and that, of course, was to remove Stanley's car.

In keeping with the military principles established over the centuries of feuding tribes and countries, I reasoned that the only possible way of saving our honourable leader's flagship from imminent capture was to set up a diversionary action.

I gunned the motor-cycle to the centre of the street, and stalled it, just as they, in the truck, were about to pass. The truck went on the brakes.

''ere!' shouted a big bastard with red cheeks and fat forearms. 'Can't you get that fugging fing out the way?'

'I'm sorry?' I said looking up from the fiddling I was doing underneath the fuel tank.

'You will be if you don't fugging move it.'

The truck driver's mate liked that one, he was grinning away and congratulating his friend on the piercing quality of his wit as I called the boss on the radio, and warned him. The driver sounded his horn and it was limp-sounding.

'I'll be out of your way in a minute,' I told him.

'Fuggin' better be, 'unt.'

Stanley came rushing out the building and leapt into his car and started it before the wardens had a chance to leave their vehicle, and accost him. Miraculously, the motor-cycle started on the first kick. I slipped it into gear and rode away, watching in the mirror, as the wardens in the van pointed to the roof for the benefit of the drivers in the truck. There was a lot of roof top watching and frantic gestures as I leant the motor-cycle over to negotiate the bend at the end of the street.

Later, I spoke with Stanley on the radio.

'Dat's good of you, James,' he said. 'I appreciate dat, and I want you to comm for a drink widd I tomorra'.'

'I'd like that, Stanley.'

'Good, good,' Stanley said. 'I an' I want you to comm wiv' me to my clobb and meet a few people.'

'I'd like that.'

'Good.'

20

'What d'you think I should wear?' I asked Pook.

'Aren't you coming to the parents' thing?' he said as he stood in the bathroom with me on the following evening.

'What thing?'

'Their anniversary party.'

'It's tonight?'

'Yeah, I told you about it weeks ago. So did they.'

'Where are they?'

'They're already there, getting it all sorted out.'

'I thought it was next week.'

'It's tonight, James, and if you don't show, they're going to be furious.'

'Damn.'

'What are you going to do?'

'I'll come afterwards.'

'Well where is this place you're going?'

'Stanley said it was in Brixton.'

'Where's that?'

'Over the river.'

'What type of club is it?'

'I don't know.'

'You'd better wear a tie for their party, James. Otherwise you won't get in,' said Pook.

It was cold in the shade, but the sun was still in the sky, and riding over Vauxhall, with the sun out and shining, my windbreaker was warmed with it, flapping in the speed of the wind as I rode. There was traffic on both banks of the river, and on the river tugs were straining with long lines of container barges. I parked my motor-cycle next to Stanley's car in a small back street in Brixton.

'What kind of machine is dat?' Stanley asked as I got off.

'It's an Lc three fifty.'

'Nice, nice. Lock it.'

I twisted the forks, so they were in full lock and turned the key all the way round in the ignition switch to engage the lock. We walked down a narrow stairway to the basement of a dilapidated building and heard from inside this wall bursting rhythm music trying to escape from behind the closed doors.

It was dark and loud in the first corridor, where the blacks with the dreadlocks stood smoking, filling the passageway with this sweet smelling smoke. Stanley was a mightily popular gentleman in the bowels of this building, shaking them all by the hand, in turn, with a handshake that had more possible combinations than the safe at the Bank of England.

I was walking behind watching them watching me feeling a little unsure of myself and not at all certain that this was a safe place for old whitey to be poking his nose.

What red eyes those gentlemen have, I was thinking, and what big white teeth, and what long, curly-matted, thick hair is hanging from their scalps and certainly they are not pleased to have such a pale face walking in their club. And boy, perhaps you should turn around and go see your mother and your father like a good boy, before they eat you.

'You wanna' drink?' Stanley shouted above all the music that was throbbing down the corridor from a room adjoining it.

What are you going to do? If you go, it's rude. If you stay, you might never go.

'Yes please,' I mumbled, not wishing to attract too much attention.

'Whaat?' he screamed back from a little way ahead.

Don't let him get too far ahead. You'll never see him again if you lose him, it's too dark.

'I'll have the same as you!' I shrieked and edged closer, smiling like a bastard. I'm a friendly whiteman, yes sir, I'm here on peaceful purposes.

We pushed our way past into the room at the end of the corridor that was large and filled with dancing people, and moved across the floor to the bar on the other side. There was an old woman serving behind a makeshift bar – a tressle top table with liquor bottles standing, and plastic cups lying, on the wet wood surface. Stanley bought the drinks. He gave me one.

I drank from the cup and the liquid was dark and sweet and warm.

'What is it?'

'Rum an' black.'

'It tastes good.'

We drank it down and had two more drinks, both of which Stanley bought, before the feeling of being nervous started to ebb away. It was difficult to talk with the noise of the music; we stood and we watched everybody dance and I did a lot of smiling.

'You see that boy dancin' with his face smiling at the chest of the woman with the God gifted breasts?'

I looked to the area that Stanley was indicating.

'Over dere, by that column t'ing.'

'Yes.'

'Dat's my cousin Jingles. Jingles!' Stanley shouted, cupping his hands over his mouth. Jingles was too engrossed in his subject to hear any of Stanley's calls.

'I get him.'

Stanley went off, apologising to all those swaying and perspiring figures whose muses he had interrupted, had a word in Jingles's ear and they started to make their way back across the dance-floor.

'Sensi, geezer?' A man with dreadlocks and a fine multi-coloured bowler hat asked me.

'No thanks.'

The bowler hat man disappeared back into the crowd, and I noticed that he was smoking a large conical shaped joint. Then I noticed that most of the others standing around, were also smoking these things.

'This is Jingles,' Stanley said.

'Pleased to meet you, Jingles.'

'All right?'

We shook hands, then we shook wrists, then forearms and finally elbows. Jingles was tall and smiling, and wore a baseball cap back to front on his head, and training shoes with monstrous red laces.

'You want to know why he called what he is?' Stanley said, tilting his head in our direction.

'Yes.'

'Must you tell everybody this story?' Jingles asked. 'You always tell it. Tell a different one.'

'I like this story, be quiet.'

Jingles turned his back on us and leaned up against a supporting column.

'When he was little, I had to babysit him for my sister,' Stanley said. 'The boy would eat anything, anyt'ing at all. One day I'm round d'ere sittin' on the couch, watchin' TV and the boy is wid' me and without my knowledge he is eatin' me bus fare home, ya know, as the money falls out of my pocket. I see him eatin' somt'in' out of the corner of me eye, but me want to watch television because, you know, John Wayne bein' attacked by the most angry bunch of shoutin', screamin', rifle-shootin' Indians you ever seen. Properly outnumbered he was. So the boy keep eatin' and John Wayne keep shootin' away at all them circlin' Indians as de fire arrows come a-burnin' and a-tearin' at the wagon train . . .'

'Haven't you finished yet?' Jingles interrupted.

'Quiet . . . as de fire arrows come a-burnin' and a-tearin' at the wagon train and den, all of a sudden, the cavalry comes chargin' down the hillside and ol' John is congratulated like a hero by all the women an' men in the train, so I turn aroun' to de boy, an' watch me last penny disappear in his mouth. I check my pockets, no money. I check his mouth, no money. I turn him upside down and shake him, an' wha'appen?'

'He threw up?'

'Not'in' 'appen! No money; but he make a right jinglin' sound. So I t'ink to meself, the boy's name must be Jingles. I tell me sister that story when she come 'ome and ever since, he been call Jingles.'

'That's a good story.' I said.

'I like it too,' Stanley said, and started chuckling. 'You want another drink?'

'Please,' I said.

'Jingles?'

'One more would be good, Stanley.'

'Three rum an' blacks,' Stanley ordered.

With the drinks, we stood away from the bar. There was a long line waiting. Stanley rolled a joint.

I watched him smoke. He was a very good smoker, and when he drew on the joint, the smoking red cherry moved inwards and Stanley's cheeks went in and out, like bellows working a fire. After he had drawn as much as he could take, Stanley opened his mouth and let the smoke run, going up his lip to his nose. Next, he threw his head back and closed his eyes. He held the joint out for Jingles and didn't exhale. Jingles took it and smoked it and gave it to me. I took it and drew on it and it burned hot in my throat as I inhaled and tried to hold it in but couldn't and let it out, coughing and coughing more. Then there was a whole lot of smoke and for a moment I couldn't see anything – it was just like opening the door of a badly smoking chimney – and when the smoke had cleared, Stanley had the biggest smile on him.

It went round like this for many goes – them smoking

professionally and me smoking and coughing and blowing it out and all of us feeling a little better for it.

I don't know how long we were in there, smoking and drinking, but when we got out it was dark and cold. There was a good bit of merriment going on and all of us were giggling – though Stanley's giggle was more like rolling thunder than giggling. It didn't take much to get a person going, either. Stanley's car was a good joke, Jingles's name was a knee slapper and my last name had us in creases. Then we heard the cats.

I didn't reckon they were that far off, a couple of streets at the most. But those cats were making an awful row and Stanley said, 'Cats,' and he suddenly stopped giggling and looked about, 'I hate dem. Dem always fytin' late in the night when a man be wantin' some sleep. Come, we mosst hunt 'em.'

So, on account of Stanley's extreme dislike for cats, we armed ourselves with small stones found in the gutter and we set off, with Stanley leading me and Jingles who were giggling. We traced the sound to an alleyway and stalked down it.

'Shhh!' said Stanley making more noise than any of the giggling we were doing. We stopped outside the backyard of a house that lay in the dark.

'There,' said Stanley. 'Dey be in dere.'

I didn't think old Stanley was right, they sounded further down to me, but as those cats weren't making any noises I wasn't sure. Well Stanley didn't wait for our opinion on the matter and heaved a handful of stones over the fence. All the stones went flying against a steel dustbin and the dustbin sang out. I didn't see any cats and I was watching very closely.

'Dey're dere,' said Stanley nodding his head. 'You try,' and I did so that they peppered the dustbin, making a terrible racket. Jingles loved that and rolled around the floor laughing away. Suddenly a light goes on in the house, on the first floor, and the window opened. Then this man started screaming at us and we tore off as fast as we could, laughing all the time. When we got back to where the car and my motor-cycle were parked we all had a terrible hunger on us.

'What are you goin' to cook us, Stanley?' said Jingles.

But old Stanley didn't seem to want to cook us anything and sighed a lot and mentioned how mad his wife was going to be with him being so late and everything and how he thought it would be a terrible thing if we were to go back to his house and face his angry woman.

'A'right,' said Jingles. 'I understand. Then you and me'll eat.'

'Where?' said I. 'I don't have any money.'

Jingles said I wouldn't need any money where we were going and so I gave him the other helmet that I still had, Chopper's spare, and we said goodbye to Stanley and I thanked Stanley an awful lot for the drinks, too much probably, and as we were leaving he told me I'd better not be late for work in the morning. Then we left.

I must say I wasn't the best of drivers and if it weren't for Jingles's belligerent nature and his wild gesticulations, we might not have got to Victoria.

'This is it,' said Jingles indicating the Supersave supermarket.

'But you have to pay in there Jingles,' said I as I rolled the machine back against the curb.

'No, you don't pay in supermarkets, fool.'

It was a shock walking into a place that was as well lit as that place was after all the darkness we'd been in for the last few hours.

'Everything a man could eat and more,' said Jingles tearing open a packet of biscuits and eating one. We got ourselves a trolley and slowly made our way up and down the aisles studying the nutritional value of different foods. These were complicated decisions made more complicated by the similarity of the names of the additives to fatal diseases often responsible for annihilating colonies of cotton tail rabbits. Once it had been established that neither of us had the blood of cotton tails in our veins – a lot had been smoked – two packages of the same food were plucked from the shelf. One was deposited in the trolley, pushed in front of myself as camouflage and decoy, and the other went in one of our pockets. As there weren't too many people in the supermarket it was not difficult sneaking them inside our coats though we were always on the lookout for the video cameras and the security guard who was prowling around.

About twenty minutes later we had managed to sift through half the shelves in the shop, when the security guard comes walking towards us. I warned Jingles and he said not to worry, act natural. I put another pack of ham in my pocket.

''ere,' cried a deep and gruff voice from the end of the aisle. 'Can I 'ave a word with you boys?'

Not knowing what to do, but thinking it would be best to keep quiet and watch Jingles for a signal to flee, I said nothing and pretended nothing had been said. Jingles said:

'You talkin' to me?'

The guard walked up and said, 'Yes sir.' I sneaked a look at him and he was one big bastard dressed in a creased blue uniform.

'What d'you want?' said Jingles curtly.

'What have you got in your coat?' the guard asked.

'What?' Jingles shouted at the guard in a voice that made the guard jump and an old lady, standing nearby, turn and stare.

The guard cleared his throat and said, 'What's in your coat, sir?'

Well I thought old Jingles would take to his heels at this point, so I slid my foot under the rear wheel of the trolley just in case the guard should push the trolley in his path – if he did run. But Jingles had no intention of running.

'*Who*', he shouted, '*the fuck d'you think you are*, asking me a question like that?'

The guard gulped and had a look around the supermarket to make sure no one was looking, and everybody was. Jingles went on:

'You think that because of the colour of my skin that I am a thief. Don't you?'

'Sir, I don't want . . .'

'*Don't you?* I'm going to tell you something. I am sick of it. You know why? I'll tell you why. You don't ask him,' and I was indicated, 'nor her, and I'll bet she's got a week's supplies in that coat of hers. No, you won't ask any of them because they are white and it's always the black man that's first under suspicion. Look at him, you say, he's a black bastard. I bet he's up to no good. See if he's got anything on him, he's bound to, all them niggers steal. So you go up to the black and you tap him on the shoulder in the middle of the shop, in front of everybody, embarrassing him in the company of his own friends. No "would you mind coming this way sir?" No, nothing like that. You got no respect, fuck you. Get me the manager. *Now!*'

This was an admirable display, I thought, and one that had wrongfooted the guard. But it did not have the desired effect of sending him scuttling off to get the manager. I also noticed that the tills had stopped ringing and I felt all the eyes in the shop on us.

'You think I'm playing?' said Jingles. 'You want to see what I do when I play? I can show you if you like but it'd be a lot easier if you went and got the manager. A lot less mess. Understand?'

The guard just looked at him. Then he looked at me and I looked him right back.

'I said, *do you understand?*' Jingles shouted.

The guard knew that leaving us was not a good idea, but he was also wise enough to realise there was no telling what this deranged black gentleman might do, if he didn't. He walked away, watching us.

Without moving his lips Jingles said, 'Run!' and we did, like hares, vaulting over the chain by the till and screaming as we ran. This scattered all the remaining shoppers in the store. We managed to lose the guard by the time we had reached the motor-cycle and later we were eating our sandwiches on a bench on Park Lane.

There was something special about those sandwiches and we guzzled the whole lot in no time at all with not a word being spoken.

After we had finished the sandwiches and the chocolate and the biscuits and the yoghurt and the apples we talked a bit. Jingles said he was a car thief but wasn't too good at it at the moment and kept getting caught. I'd never spoken to a car thief before so I asked him how it was being a car thief and he said it was fine if you could do it properly. He said a man could make a pretty good wage from it and that's hard nowadays. I agreed with him. He told me how you break into cars and how you start them and who buys them and everything. I asked him why he did it and he said he had a family and the dole just didn't pay enough. So I said that was fair enough too and we sat back on the bench and had a smoke.

Then I remembered trouble.

'Jingles,' I said. 'What time is it?'

He said it must be after eleven and so I started fidgeting wondering what to do about the parents' party. If I went they would be none too pleased about me bringing Jingles along but if I didn't take him I'd probably never see him again and after all the fun we'd had that evening that seemed like a shame, so I asked him if he wanted to come along and he said, 'You bet, I love parties.' So we went.

The party was being held in this place called Sissy's – a

place that you can rent and it's big and grand with sweeping staircases and opulent pictures and red carpets everywhere. It had everything you'd want for a grand party including butlers and maids to wait on the guests and when we arrived there we met a frog on the doorstep. He was a little big for a frog and he stood on two legs, but the colour of his skin was the same. The frog was the doorman and Jingles said when we were walking up and after we had noted his resemblance to frogs in general, 'If the man is a frog in disguise, he's a fool. There ain't no princess that's goin' to kiss a face like that.'

And Jingles was right, the frog was none too pretty.

'Evenin',' said the doorman. 'What d'you want?'

I straightened myself up and told him that we were invited but he didn't believe it. I think it might have had something to do with the way we were dressed, not being in black tie and everything. Then a big fat Roller pulled up at the curb and we turned and Jingles said.

'Look at that, Jimmy, Rol-l-s-Royce. Sweet, oh ver' sweet.'

We sort of stood around on the side and watched as a little chauffeur ran around to open the door. At first we couldn't see who it was but then we were presented with a huge pair of enormous buttocks hideously deformed by a very tight pair of knickers and shrouded in black lace. We saw a stilettoed heel make careful contact with the red carpet and then the doorman advanced. There was a whole lot of muffled squealing going on inside and we heard the strains of a strained conversation. This was followed by a piercing shriek, the flesh on flesh sound of a striking hand and finally we saw a flurry of tail shaking activity as the poor lady tried to disengage herself from whatever or whoever it was that sat in the darkness of the tinted glass limousine.

The doorman offered his hand as the lady straightened herself, still with her back to us and breathing heavily. She ignored his offer of gallantry and concentrated her efforts on patching those areas of pudgy white flesh that should have been covered by her dress, but weren't. Then, once upright, she realised that her hair that had once been arranged in the most regal of buns now lay in ruins. We watched as it was restored to some of its former glory by a rigorous attack with hairpins.

'That pussy's big,' said Jingles. 'You know her?'

'I'm not sure.'

Just then Pook came skittling out of the building, all breathless, saw us and went up to the doorman and said, 'It's all right doorman, sir, he's my brother.' Suddenly the lady turned round and said, in the most delighted of tones, 'Pook! What a surprise!'

Pook froze and when he'd finished doing that he cried, 'Oh my God, Lucy!' and turned and fled indoors.

Lucy came over to us followed by this small man who had just got out of the car. He was adjusting himself.

'James,' old Luce said, 'how delightful to see you. How are you?'

'Very well thank you, Lucy.'

We kissed and Lucy had a good look over Jingles.

'This is Jingles,' I said. 'Jingles, this is Lucy.'

'Nice,' said Jingles and they shook and after, we went inside. The reception hall was packed and everybody wore a suit, except myself and Jingles.

'Who is your friend, Lucy?' I asked.

'Didn't I introduce you? How silly of me. This is Baron.'

'Baron who?' said I.

'No idea, darling. I simply call him Baron. He answers to that name you know.'

'Pleased to meet you Baron,' I said holding out my hand. Baron spoke with a funny accent – I think it might have been German – and he said, 'No. It ees my pleysure.'

'No it's my pleasure,' said I. 'You don't know what a

service you are doing for the family going out with this lady. I want you to meet a good friend of mine. Jingles, this is Baron, Baron, this is Jingles.'

Jingles gave the man one of his more complicated hand-shakes which I think he liked as he smiled and then demanded that they do it again and again so that the Baron could learn 'zis straaange cuustom'. After three attempts, the Baron had the shake all the way down to the last finger-ful and was so pleased that he shouted, 'Das is good, jah!' clapped Jingles on the shoulder and led him off to the stairs in search of 'vodka'.

'Drink, sir, madame?' asked a young wine waiter. I lifted two glasses of champagne from the silver tray and handed one to Lucy.

'Where did you find him, Luce?'

'Oh, some club or other.'

'Was he the man you were talking about with mother in the kitchen, when I was there?'

'Yes.'

'What's he do?'

'He doesn't. His family is far too rich to work.'

'He seems like a nice man.'

'Oh he is, darling. He's sweet. Where's your brother gone?'

'No idea.'

'Shame.'

Lucy scanned the room in search of suitable prey, and seeing nothing decided that it would be more advantageous to her if she were to scale the stairs, and try again from the vantage point of the first floor. She downed her glass in one, handed it to me, and waddled off to mount the sweep-ing staircase.

'Drink, sir?' the wine waiter asked.

I replaced both glasses on the tray, after finishing the small amount that lay in the bottom of my glass, and took a full glass.

'Darling! How simply wonderful to see you!' cried a familiar voice from above. I turned and looked upwards to see Mother and old Lucy embracing on the landing above, and remembering that I had failed to wear a tie, quickly scurried away through the drinking masses and sought refuge in a small room off the main hall.

The room was as grand as all the others, just smaller. On the walls there were portraits in oils of celebrated ladies and gentlemen of the Victorian era, wisely framed in glass, dressed in their Sunday Best and standing in all sorts of contrived and pompous poses. The glass was there as protection to ensure that the paintings weren't damaged by the over zealous behaviour of the often very drunk guests. On one of the walls, I spotted a beautiful young lady carrying a parasol and wearing a hat. She was walking in front of the Eiffel Tower. Her height and shape were almost identical to our very own sweet Marie. Yes, the swollen lower lip was identical and so too was the coy expression on her face. But where was Marie? Perhaps she is helping at the bar. No, she's not there. Then upstairs, maybe.

'Good evening, James.'

I tured to face Mrs Crackington-Smythe, an old warhorse, and mother of ex-school companion, Cyril.

'Good evening. How are you?' I said smiling.

'Oh very well, thank you. And how are you?'

'Fine, thank you.'

'Cyril tells me you are no longer at um . . .'

'Yes, he's right; old Mum and Dad simply couldn't afford to pay the fees any more so I'm working as a despatch rider to help contribute.'

'Champagne, madame, sir?' said the wine waiter. We drank our glasses and took two refills.

'Really? Well Cyril thinks he might like to have a go at it this summer. He's frightfully clever at finding his way round all those confusing little mewses in Eaton Square.'

'I'm sure he'll be well suited to the job, then.'

'D' you think so?'

'Certainly.'

I drank from my glass.

'Well, tell me where you went today.'

'Catford, Lewisham, East Grinstead . . .'

'Where?'

'I'm sure Cyril would know. He's bound to.'

I spotted Pook circling round the room at high speed, like a drunken shark.

'Excuse me, I must have a word with my brother.'

She let me go and latched on to an old Major who was hovering near the wine waitress. I intercepted Pook on his third circle of the room. When I grabbed him, he started giggling. He was gone.

'Are you all right?' I said. He giggled again. 'What have you been drinking?'

'Orange juice,' he slurred. 'Best tasting orange juice I've ever had.'

'You been drinking that Bucks Fizz stuff?'

'Nope, just this fizzy Fanta stuff. Makes you feel pretty strange.'

'I better take you home.'

'No. I don't want to go home. I like it here. Say, where's Lucy?'

'You don't want to know that. She'd murder you if she saw you in the state you're in.'

'I know that. I just need to know where she is so I don't bump into her. That's all.'

'You'll be all right in here, but don't drink any more. You understand?'

'I understand,' said Pook and he hiccupped. I let him go and as soon as he was released he started to circle the room in ever widening circles, slipping in and out of the talking guests like a slalom skier might negotiate a course of poles. I was on my way out of the room, when I heard a squawk, followed, almost immediately, by the words, '*You little brute!*' It had to be Pook, I thought. There was no other explanation, unless, of course, old Baron had snuck into the room and attacked somebody from the rear. When I turned, I saw that little drunken Pook had missed one of the gates, and instead, had rammed it. Mrs Crackington-Smythe was the gate. She was wearing her drink.

'I think I'd better come with you, James,' said Pook as he came rushing towards me.

'Yes, I think you'd better.'

'Where are you going?'

'To the gents.'

'Good, she can't get me in there.'

We hurried back through the reception area and followed the signs to the gents, in the basement. There was a powerful smell of grass as we walked in.

'Jingles, is that you?'

'Yeah Jimmy, come on in.'

'Where are you?'

'Over 'ere.'

Away from the main urinal, there was a small partition and a door. This room housed the boiler, Jingles and the drunken Baron. We went in.

'Marie, what are you doing in here?' I asked, for I had not seen her when I opened the door.

'Your friend Jeengels and the Baron invited me.'

'Oh, good. Good,' I said. 'And how are you, Baron?'

'I am good,' said the Baron. 'I have been telling your young friends about my car collection. It seems that Jingles also collects cars, is that not so, Jingles?'

'Only the best ones, Baron.'

'Me too,' said the Baron.

'Say, what kind of cars d'you have, Baron?' said Pook.

'All sorts. Racing cars, limousines, coupés. I have your friend here coming round to see me next week, to help start an old Rolls of which I have lost the keys many years.'

'Are you sure about that, Baron,' I said. 'I thought you and Lucy were going away together next week.'

'No, no. Jingles said he can start any car because he thieves them. I invited him to come thieve my Rolls for me. It's so charming, n'est-ce pas?'

'Are you a car thief?' Pook asked.

'Sometimes.'

'Oh yeah? Will you teach me, will ya?'

Jingles exhaled a large plume of smoke and passed me the joint, grinning.

''ees so sweet,' said Marie. 'Such a leetle deville.' Pook went up to Marie and gave her a big hug.

'So tell me, Baron, how d'you know old Lucy?' I asked.

'Lucy?' said the Baron. 'She ees magnificent, isn't she? Such a fine figure and so strong! I met her at this club, you know. I was seeting on a stool with a little glass in front and she came across and tells something and I think it is not for me and next fing I know, Kaboom!'

'Kaboom?' said Jingles.

'Yes, Kaboom! And I am lying on the floor in confusion.'

'Confusion or concussion?' I ask.

'Yes, both, and so, I look up to see what it is that hit me and there she is, enormous, wonderful, Lucy! And she ees sitting on my stool, laughing. Ah! How she ees magnificent! I love her!'

'That's great, Baron. I think you'll be very happy together. She's a great lady, she's got a lot of drive.'

'Drive!' said the Baron. 'Good. Then we won't have to put the car on the train to go the South of France!'

'That wasn't quite what I meant, but I'm sure she can anyway. Here, have some of this.'

The Baron took the joint and starting sucking on it, with both of his hands wrapped around, making two fists, one on top of the other, with the joint sticking out of the bottom fist and drawing the smoke up into the top fist and then into his mouth.

'Where did you learn to do that?' Jingles asked.

'My father, he smoked peace pipes with the Indians, you know, in the last century. He was in Canada prospecting for gold. He taught me,' said the Baron as he took another hit.

'Be careful, Baron,' said Jingles. 'It isn't tobacco.'

The Baron kept on sucking and exhaling at the joint like a man smoking at a pipe. Finally he let his hands fall, looked up towards the ceiling and let all the smoke come rushing out of him. His eyes were bulging in their sockets.

'What d'you think, Baron?' said Jingles.

'That's some wacky tobaccy,' said the Baron.

Later, we were all upstairs on the first landing where most of the guests had now congregated to witness my mother and father dancing alone in the middle of the dance floor. They were dancing to this waltz tune. Pook, myself, Marie and Jingles stood by the entrance to the room underneath the chandelier. The good Baron and Miss Lucy were opposite. Old Lucy was dabbing at her eyes with her handkerchief and the Baron was grinning like a monkey. The tune went on, and Mum led Dad around the room and they were both smiling, but I could see my old father's eyes were taking an unusual amount of interest in our section of the room. Each time they circled in front of us, Pook sang out some form of drunken encouragement and Dad would glare. I was pretty sure I was going to be blamed for Pook's condition. Then, there was also the consideration of the missing tie and the uninvited guest.

When the dance was over, there was all sorts of drunken applause from the friends, relatives and business associates gathered. The disc jockey put on a popular record and soon the whole floor was covered with writhing bodies.

'Champagne, madame, sirs?' asked the wine waiter.

'Thank you,' I said and took one and passed one to Marie and the other to Jingles.

'D'you have any of that orange juice stuff?' Pook asked.

'Yes, sir,' said the wine waiter.

'No! Pook, you can't have another. You'll be sick.'

'Aww c'mon, James.'

'No.'

The wine waiter moved away.

'Look at old Lucy move!' said Pook pointing across the floor. He was right, she could move and so was everybody else – in the opposite direction. Lucy was performing, spinning round and round with increasing velocity, whilst the good Baron did his best to follow her on the floor, ducking each time one of Lucy's outstretched arms came scything through the air, ready to decapitate anything in its path. Fortunately for the survivors on the dance floor, the record finally played out the last few chords, leaving Lucy breathless, and the Baron weeping with joy at the sight of such a devastating creature making such an impact in so small a place. The next record started, and the Baron led Lucy away from the floor to a secluded table at the far end of the room. There was an audible sigh of relief from those victims on the dance floor that were spared an encore of Lucy's holocaustic behaviour.

'Champagne, madame, sirs?'

'Thank you.'

'Eh mister! Have you got any rum an' blacks?' Jingles said.

The waiter smiled and walked away.

There was some champion dancing being danced on the floor. One man, a tall man with a rose stuck behind his ear, now dishevelled in appearance, was stalking the flashing lights of the disc jockey's box like a lepidopterist might hunt a prize specimen butterfly.

Another gentleman, undoubtedly a fan of Jesus Christ's, stood in the crucifix position in the middle of the floor, humming. Not many people paid much attention to him. Then, something terrible happened. Jingles asked Marie if she would dance with him. Something worse followed: she accepted. They went out onto the floor leaving me alone with a sleeping Pook. I was terribly jealous.

'More champagne, sir?'

I took two and watched. It was a miserable sight. Old Jingles was a killer dancer, he must have had rubber in his bones or something, because he made all these impressive torso twisting spins and shakes and jerks, and Marie lapped it up. She loved it, she really did. I could see from where I was that she had this big, dopey grin on her face. She was completely ready to melt for him. I hated watching it; I tried watching old rose-behind-the-ear, but the eyes kept wandering back, and each time they wandered back, Jingles and Marie would be dancing a little closer together. What made it worse was that she was copying him. Everything he did, she would do. He shook his waist and sure enough, she'd shake her waist. He shook his chest and, believe me, when she shook her chest, it shook.

Now, what I should have done, was to go and dance alongside them, and show how great I was at dancing. Then, old Marie would have been mightily impressed and shaken some of it at me. But I didn't. I couldn't, I'm a lousy dancer. God put bricks in my blood, not rhythmn in my bones. This has to be one of the principal reasons for my consistently terrible and failed attempts at going out with girls for a period of longer than a week.

Sometimes, it doesn't even last a week. Friday will come along, the girl will want to go dancing at some wonderfully chic-chic nightclub, I won't, she'll go, and invariably she will be picked up by some highly wonderful pelvic thruster who loves Mr James Brown. They dance to his record, 'Sex Machine', him shaking it all in front of her, and bang! She's gone. When I ring up the following morning, the mother answers the phone and I ask to speak to the daughter. The mother then asks my name, I tell her. I hear the mouthpiece being sheltered, my name being uttered, and the mother comes back on the phone to say that the daughter has gone out and won't be back until much later.

I thank her and don't bother calling again.

Once, I even went so far as to sign up for this dance class thing. I think the name of the place was Madame Beasly's School of Dance. I signed up for a whole two months of lessons. On my very first lesson, I realised that I had made a terrible mistake. I was pretty terrific at the steps they taught, but unfortunately it wasn't modern dance. If I had taken the things I had learned and tried them out in a night-club there would not be one girl in the whole place that would want to dance with me.

I was much better at the tango than the foxtrot, though I was pretty excellent at the rumba and it was the rumba that was my favourite. However, there weren't many places you can go rumbaling. The only places you can are strictly for O.A.P.s. I went once, though, just to see how it was. I took a girl called Franny Roper or Roper the Groper as she was called at one of my schools. I thought I'd impress her with my wonderful dancing. She hated it, and left twenty minutes after we had arrived. It was a shame, we could have had a great evening. Instead, I ended up dancing with this huge blonde divorcee from Streatham, a lady by the name of Phyllis. We danced two dances together and at the end of the second, I had to retire hurt. The lady tried to dance like the sugar plum fairy; that, she said, was her aim. In fact, her aim was little closer to home; it was more like a bulldozer. That is what it was like dancing with Phyllis. My fingers ached and my toes were swollen for days.

'Champagne, sir?'

'Thank you.'

The room had emptied. Jingles and Marie were dancing all close and so were the Baron and Lucy. Rose-behind-the-ear and the Jesus imposter had become very friendly and were escorting each other around the room, explaining and demonstrating to each other, their separate, and highly individual, ritualised dances.

167

'James, we would like a word with you.'

I turned around and Mum and Dad were right behind me.

'Of course, what is it?' I said.

'We'd like you to come with us for a second, to somewhere a little more secluded,' Dad said.

'Can't you say it here?'

'No.'

'All right.'

We went downstairs to the cloakroom. The attendant had gone home.

'James, you are not wearing a tie,' Mother said.

'Is that what you wanted to tell me?'

'No,' said Dad.

'Why aren't you wearing a tie, James?' Mother said.

'What d'you want to tell me?' I said.

'Why aren't you wearing a tie, James?' Mother repeated.

'We will find out in a minute, dear,' said Dad. 'Now who is he, James?'

'Who?'

'Your friend, the black boy.'

'Why aren't you wearing a tie, James?' said mother, persisting in her quest.

'Darling, please,' Dad pleaded. 'Important things first. Now James, tell me . . .'

'This *is* important, dear. Why aren't you wearing your tie?'

'Are you drunk, Mother?'

'Tell me!' she demanded.

'I forgot, sorry,' I said.

'You forgot! Our very own son forgets to wear a tie on our twenty-fifth wedding anniversary. It's disgraceful!'

'I'm sorry, Mother,' I said.

'Who is he, James?' said Dad.

'His name's Jingles.'

'We didn't ask you to invite him, James.'

'I know.'

'Why did you bring him?'

'Because he's a friend.'

'Darling, our own son didn't wear a tie this evening. It's too much!' said Mother.

'I know dear,' said Father. 'You should have worn a tie James, you know how much it means to your mother for you to make an effort on a simple family occasion like this. There is no excuse. We don't want him here either.'

'Who, Jingles?'

'Yes.'

'Why not?'

'Darling, he didn't wear a tie!' Mother said.

'I know dear,' said Dad.

'Why not?' I asked again.

'Because, he wasn't invited.'

'Are you sure that's the reason? Or is it the excuse?'

'What d'you mean?' said my father.

'You know what I mean. If Jingles were a John or a James I'm sure it would not have mattered. You'd have ignored it.'

'We're not racist, James.'

'Oh no? So where are all your black friends? I don't see any.'

'That is not the point, James. He was not invited. Now kindly tell him to leave.'

'I won't. He's my friend. I invited him.'

'Either you tell him to leave or you don't come home this evening.'

'Is that a threat?'

'It's no threat, James. It is the way it is.'

'Fine. I won't come home.'

I left, then, and went outside as quick as I could and felt rotten about having disappointed them on so special an occasion. Not wearing a tie was something I should have done but forgot to do and there wasn't really any excuse. But the business about Jingles – that was stupid and it didn't seem right that they should get so het up about that and that made me boil.

I got on my motor-cycle and just rode and when I was riding I felt that chances were against me not getting stopped and breathalysed having drunk so much. So I started thinking where I could go and thought about going to see old Joan but I decided against that one, with it being two thirty in the morning. So I went up to the park to see if I could find the ducks.

The park was shut and I had to leave my motor-cycle in the carpark at Bowater House and climb over the iron gates. Once I was in the park I wasn't at all sure about this idea and started to get a little spooked by the dark. I don't know what it is but the dark makes great food for the imagination and in no time at all I was thinking about the freaks that go up to the park at night to roam about and mug the odd person. I started seeing people in trees, so I crept about the place staying well in the shadows. I imagined all sorts of things and none of them were too healthy. I could see the papers in the morning with a story about me being dead and then I saw all the family standing around sobbing and that was a comforting thought.

I got up to the Serpentine and I was still in one piece but I was still nervous, though I no longer felt drunk – the fear had drained that. I walked about and there were no ducks to be seen. I could see most things now that the clouds had cleared and the moon was shining. I could see right the way to the other side of the park, maybe a mile or so away, to Marble Arch, and I could see the boathouse across the water as clear as you'd like. The wind was rustling up in the tree-tops and every now and then a horn would go off in the distance. It was pretty lonesome up there in the park at that hour.

I thought I heard something behind me and so I started

running and didn't stop until I was over the other side of the lake, near the boathouse. I was out of breath, then, and when I looked back I couldn't see anyone, but I felt somebody was there, watching. Maybe it was my imagination but I didn't want to risk it and didn't think the idea too dandy of being tomorrow's news. I didn't know what to do, my hands were shaking and I could feel my heart pounding. Then I had the idea of going into the boathouse, so I snuck round the back, out of sight of whoever it was, and slid along the railings over the water and then, when I got to the end of the wall, I climbed up and over the wooden gates and dropped down onto the dock as quiet as I could.

I felt a little safer inside with the boats being there and having a wall around me and a roof and I decided that if I heard him coming along the outside of the wall, I'd slip into the water and swim under the gates and away, still holding my breath, and he would never catch me. So I settled down in one of the boats underneath the tarpaulin and tried to get some sleep. But it was no good, no matter how hard I tried, and I was tired, it just wouldn't come. After a while I started to relax as the mugger hadn't come yet and I was almost falling off when I heard this sound, and it was quite frequent. It went 'splat', and then another and that went 'splat' and then another. I couldn't work it out. Then a splat fell on the tarpaulin just near my shoulder and I reached out to feel it and started thinking that maybe the mugger had somehow snuck on the roof without me knowing and was spitting on me. But he wasn't – it was duckshit. They were all here, up in the rafters, sleeping. I knew this because the texture felt different. All my friends were here and I was happy that they were, but I wasn't so pleased about what they were doing. I stayed there another twenty minutes, under the tarpaulin, then I had to get out. It was like Chinese water torture.

I snuck out and then made a bolt for the cover of some

trees away to the right and when I got there, I climbed one and stayed up there in the branches, away from the freaks, until the sun came up. I would have gone home but there was no way I was going to walk back through the park. So I stayed and I shivered and waited.

21

For the next couple of days, I slept all over the place. Stanley let me sleep in the office; I stayed with Rita and Frank at the squat they lived in near Kew; I even slept in the garden opposite the flat in Sloane Street, in the sandpit. I talked to the parents on the phone and they said it would be fine for me to come home, but, to tell you the truth, I didn't really want to any more. For the first couple of nights I was desperate to get back to my bed, my brother, my dog, and a fridge full of food. But afterwards I began thinking that it would be better for all if I left home for the summer and found somewhere else to live. Rent was not a problem with the money I was earning from Rocket but I had no idea where to look or where I wanted to live. Then, fortune smiled on me when Frank told me that Wilco, a rider who had been hospitalised since I first arrived at Rocket, was not coming back to live with them at the squat, and there would be a vacancy. I said I'd like to move in and he said that would be fine. I moved in the following Saturday.

I had been home a couple of times since the evening of the anniversary for changes of clothes and my washbag. I had to enter the house by the roof and my bedroom window. Now, on Saturday, I was home packing my bags and Norman was waiting outside in the transit he had borrowed.

'You don't have to go, James,' Mother said.

'I know.'

'Well why don't you stay, darling, and cut out this nonsense?'

'No, I think it would be better if I went.'

'Your father didn't mean what he meant,' said Mother.

'James,' Pook said. 'Was that a Freudian slip?'

'I think so,' I said.

'I mean your father didn't mean what he said.'

'It doesn't matter, Mother. I was wrong for bringing Jingles in any case.'

'Well, stay. Tell the boy outside to go away or, if you must, invite him in for a cup of tea.'

It was tempting, it really was. But, I had already told the others I would be moving in and it would look terrible if I changed my mind at the last minute.

'No. I'm going to go.'

'What about next term? A decision has to be made on what school you will attend.'

'We can talk about it another time.'

'I think we should talk about it now.'

'No. Another time.'

'No, James, now.'

'Let's talk about it next week.'

'No. We will talk about it now. Pook, take the dog out for a walk.'

'Why? He's just been out to the garden. Can't I stay and watch?'

'Take him out, now!' Mother barked.

'Aw mum, do I have to?'

'*Go!*' she said pointing to the bedroom door. Pook huffed and sighed a bit and then left. I said, 'I'm going now.'

'You are not,' said Mum.

'I am. I think it would be best if we finished this on another occasion.'

'No,' said Mother, shutting the door and standing in front of it.

'Yes,' said I opening it. Mother shut it. I opened it. She slammed it once more. So I gave up with the door and went to the window, opened it and climbed out before she had a chance to nab me.

'James, come back here,' she shouted. 'Right this instant!'

Well, I didn't. I went over the roof with the bag on my back and started climbing the drainpipe, and damn difficult it was too with that bag. Old mumma was not pleased and bawled away until I was at the top of the building. She was capable of being very angry indeed. I scarpered down the fire exit with haste and when I was down on the street I legged it to the van.

Later we pulled up at the end of a road of terraced houses in a cul-de-sac in Kew. The house was just like all the others, only it looked a little more festive: there were lights hanging up outside. I said to Norman, 'What are those for?' and he said that Rita wanted a mate and so she was throwing a party that evening.

'Tonight?' said I.

'Yeah, man. You're invited, Chopper's coming, all the boys are coming. You can bring anyone you want.'

'Can I?'

'Yeah.'

'Who else is coming?'

'I think she invited Daisy and his friends.'

'The Gravedigger man?'

'That's the one.'

'But he's a hoodlum,' I said.

'She don't care.'

We unloaded my bag and walked into the small garden, littered with motor-cycle parts, and rang the bell. Rita answered it and led me upstairs to the attic. The house was a complete dump. There were no carpets, curtains or lampshades, and the walls were covered with graffiti. Each room I poked my nose into had a motor-cycle in some stage of undress.

'What do you think?' said Rita.

'Lovely.'

Up in the attic there was a small window, a sloping ceiling and a single mattress on the floor. There was nothing else. No cupboard, no chest of drawers, no table, no chair – nothing.

'What happened to the furniture?'

'Wilco took it with him when he left. It was a good thing he did. We would have had to burn it. He was a filthy bastard.'

'Is the mattress bug free?' I asked.

'Yeah, it's a new one. Norman found it.'

'Where did he find it?'

'On a tip.'

'Oh good, it's legal then.'

Rita smiled and said, 'I'll leave you to it.' Rita left the room, slamming the door behind her. If there was going to be a party in the squat that evening, I reasoned that it would be best if I did not unpack. Instead, I took the bag up onto the roof and hid it behind the chimney, wedging it carefully between the roof and the chimney stack.

In the afternoon, I rang Kath, I rang Jingles and I rode to Hammersmith to buy Kath a small gift. I wanted to buy a ring but I didn't have enough money, so I bought some flowers and took them back to the squat.

Kath said she would arrive at about eight. She was a little late, she turned up and it was just after eleven. The house was packed with motor-cycle men. The street was lined with motor-cycles. Most of them were despatch bikes and not all of them came from Rocket. She came in with her cousin, a tall skinhead gentleman.

'I'm glad you could come,' I said.

'Oh hello, James,' said Kath.

'D'you want a drink? There's plenty of it over in the corner there,' I said pointing at the beer barrel standing on a table in the sitting room.

'Thanks. James. This is Johnny. Johnny's from Italy.'

176

'I didn't know they had skinheads in Italy.'

'Didn't you? Well they do.'

Johnny didn't say a word. Kath led him away to find a drink. I watched them go. She was pretty friendly with this cousin. As he poured the booze, she niggled at his ear with her finger and giggled. The man was an ape. I looked at him. He was at least six foot three in heels, so what? I think he was a mute, I didn't see him say one word. What is she doing with a mute? He had a gormless expression, probably one of the stupidest I have ever seen. It didn't seem to worry her too much. I think she liked it, she was certainly smiling enough. And look at those tattoos, what kind of fool would wear tattoos? Just look at them. Just look at what she's doing to them. Just look at the way she's running her fingers around that snake. Just look at the way she's running her fingers around that snake and up that snake and down that snake. Don't look at them.

'How are ya, Frankie old mate?' Chopper shrieked.

Frankie beckoned to us and disappeared back up the stairs. We followed. In his room, he closed the door behind us.

'What d'you think?' Frank asked.

'About what, Frank?' I said.

'The uniform over there. It's an original.'

There was a dummy standing in front of the window, an inflatable one and it was wearing a police sergeant's uniform.

'Oh Frank it's great,' I said. 'It'll definitely suit you.'

'Thanks.'

'Have you got any dope, Frank?' Chopper said.

'I have.'

'Would you roll a joint?'

'What time is it?' Frank asked.

'Eleven thirty,' I said.

'Why do you want to know the time?' Chopper asked.

'I'm on duty in two hours, I got to clean the house out. Just too many people.'

'Give us the dope,' Chopper said. 'Let me roll one.'

Frank went to his chest, under the bed, pulled out a small plastic bag and threw it to Chopper. Then he threw Chopper some papers. Chopper rolled one and lit it.

There was a terrible rumbling from out in the street. I went to the window and saw a dirty great pack of chopped motor-cycles slowly riding towards the house, their lights blazing.

'Who the hell is this?' I asked.

They came to the window and Frank said, 'That'll be Daisy and his friends.'

'You mean Rita's boyfriend?' I asked.

'That's right. He's the one with the beard, leading them.'

Each one of the riders that I could see had a beard. They rode up to the house and some rode into it.

'Why didn't they walk into the house?' Sherry asked.

'They're probably too drunk,' said Chopper.

We walked out of Frank's room to seek a better view of our new guests. Upstairs, we heard a herd of wildebeests stirring.

'Stand back!' Frank warned.

We pressed ourselves against the wall just in time to watch Rita come thundering past, raising the dust on the landing. We felt the tremors as she descended to the ground floor, crying 'Daisy! Daisy!'

We quickly hurried after her, passing the long lines of hairy heavy metal gentlemen passionately involved in head banging. Some banged the walls some banged each other. Downstairs, a silence had engulfed all of the guests. Rita stood rock still on the stairs looking at Daisy who was busy helping himself to as much beer as he could swallow. He had given up the idea of using a cup and instead, lifted the beer barrel above his head with the tap turned on, greedily guzzling at the liquid as it poured into and out of his mouth. The other members of the gang had made a slender corridor through the guests, a path by which the two lovers could meet.

'Daisy!' Rita swooned.

Daisy was more interested in satisfying his seemingly endless thirst, and carried on drinking. Rita tried again.

'Daisy!' she cried.

This time Daisy heard, and with the beer tap running, passed the barrel to his second-in-command.

'Reetah!' belched Daisy now looking her straight in the toes.

'Daisy!' squeeled Rita.

'Reetah!' Daisy bellowed. She walked towards him. He walked towards her. He fell towards her. He passed out in front of her. Rita dragged him into the back garden with the help of a couple of his hoodlums.

'Love,' Frank said. 'It's such a splendid thing.'

'You wanna dance Sherry?' Chopper asked. She said she did and they went off to shake it.

'Where's Norman?' I asked Frank.

'He's hiding. He's terrified of petal, there,' said Frank indicating a semi-conscious, pot-bellied monster disappearing from the room.

'Where's Kath?' Frank asked.

'I don't know.'

'You'd better find her, hadn't you?'

'Yup.'

I went off. I searched the kitchen and witnessed one of the Diggers giving a free demonstration on the art of bottle opening using nothing other than a thick skull. Not the Digger's skull, but a friendly head-banger's. In the bathroom one of the Diggers was giving a lecture on anatomy to a toothless woman, and in the hall, two Diggers were involved in the art of self-defence, swinging chains and breaking bottles and chairs over those who needed self-defending. Upstairs in my room, I found her. I found him with her. I found them, on my bed.

'You're in here then,' I said.

'That's right,' said Kath.

'Oh . . . What are you doing?'

'Johnny's got a headache.'

'Does he need you with him if he's got a headache? Couldn't you come downstairs for a while?' I asked.

'Piss off,' said Johnny.

'How about it?' I pleaded.

Johnny propped his ugly mug on his hand and said, 'Piss off.' He sounded English. I asked Kath again, and again the bright boy said, 'Piss off.'

Normally, in situations like these a level headed person would probably oblige. She was not making any effort to convey her wish for me to stay in the room; and as for the man Johnny, not only did he not wish for me to be in the room, but also he was making visible signs of raising his poor headache-ridden bulk from its resting place on my bed, to come give me a little help with the door. But I couldn't leave, not after all the thoughts I'd had for her.

'How would you like some aspirin?' I offered. The response was the same. I could have predicted it. Maybe he really was Italian. Maybe living in Hackney for the last week had only taught him these two words. Now, he was off the bed, he was walking towards me, I was walking backwards, there was a wall behind me, I hit it, he hit me, I hit him, we fought. I was on the floor and he was sitting on my chest with his fingers around my neck for support. I was blacking out when he suddenly slumped forward relaxing his grip, and passed out next to me.

'What happened?' I think I said.

'I hit him,' said Kath.

'Thank you,' I said massaging my neck. 'Is he dead?'

Kath rolled him over onto his back, opened an eye, and studied it. 'Nope,' she said. 'He's not dead, just sleeping.'

'What did you hit him with?' I asked.

'My bag. Are you all right?'

'Oh yeah, fine,' said I getting up and falling down.

'Here,' Kath said. 'Let me give you a hand.'

I took the hand that she gave and we went downstairs.

The rooms downstairs were shaking through a combination of music, played at a volume where the words of the singer were completely indistinguishable from the chords of his guitar, and long-haired glue sniffers banging their skulls against the walls in fervent appreciation of the din coming from the overloaded stereo system.

'I think I need some air,' I said wanting to get as far from this house as possible. 'You wanna come for a walk?'

A bottle came flying across the room and exploded on the wall behind us.

'Yes,' said Kath.

We went out of the house, and walked to the river, leaving the light of the streetlamps to walk in the darkness on the river towpath. The river was quiet and ran smoothly and full with the tide. Some ducks, disturbed by us, swam out from the bank and went with the tide, down river.

'Look,' I said. 'Ducks!'

'What is it with ducks that you like so much?' Kath asked.

'I thought I had told you.'

'You had, but I don't understand.'

'Well, it's complicated. Are you sure you want to hear it?'

'No.'

'All right.'

'Are you living in the squat?'

'Yes.'

'Poor you.'

'It's better than where I have been staying for the last week.'

'Oh?'

I told Kath about my night in the boathouse with my

friends, the ducks, sleeping above in the rafters. She seemed to enjoy the story and laughed.

'Can I ask you a question?'

'It depends on the question,' said Kath.

'That man, Johnny. He isn't your cousin, is he?'

We carried on walking in the darkness, and only very faintly could you hear the din from the house.

'Is he?'

'No.'

'D'you have a cousin from Italy?'

'Yes.'

'Is she staying with you?'

'No.'

'I see. Then he's your boyfriend?'

'Not really. He's only part-time.'

We walked under a bridge and the towpath widened.

'Are you cold? D'you want my sweater?'

Kath smiled. 'Won't you be cold?' she said.

'No, not at all. I'm hotblooded.'

'Oooh.'

'I didn't mean that. I meant I've got good circulation, that's all.'

She laughed and I felt embarrassed. I took off my sweater and gave it to her and she put it on. Being gallant was hard work: it was freezing walking along the path. My arm was covered in goose bumps. Soon, we came to a field and looking across, in the dark, I saw cows.

'Cows!' Kath said pointing.

'Where?' said I.

'Over there,' she said pointing.

'I can't see anything.'

'Over there!'

'You've got great eyesight,' said I wanting to flatter her and thinking this was the best place to start. 'There is a game you can play with sleeping cows. Farmers do it all the time.'

'What's that?'

'Cow tipping. Have you ever played it?'

'No.'

'It's a simple game, but it's no good for the animal.'

'What d'you have to do?'

'Knock 'em over.'

'The cow?'

'Yup. Because it's asleep it doesn't see you coming up, and if you knock it in the right place, it'll fall over. Then it wakes up.'

'Who plays it?'

'Farmers' boys, when they're drunk.'

'How d'you know?'

'I used to go to a school in the country. I knew all the local farmers' sons. They used to do it all the time, they had no respect for the animals. They thought it was a great joke.'

We were looking across the field, and there was a gentle wind blowing, stirring the treetops. Then Kath says, all of a sudden:

'D'you want to kiss me?'

'What?'

'D'you want to kiss me?'

'Yes. Yes, I'd like that.'

'Well go on then,' she urged closing her eyes and presenting her lips. Pinch yourself, I thought. This can't be true.

We kissed. Oh my God, what a feeling. Could make any man a champion. Could wreck the circuits on any pacemaker attached to any heart. Could send a man spiralling down into the dizzy depths of pure lust. Could make a man forget about ducks for the rest of his days. It was all of those things and more. There was warmth in that kiss, a burning warmth all over. No more goose bumps, no more worries. All was well.

That night, we did it, sort of. We tried, but I was not

very successful at docking. That part took a long time. Kath was warm and patient with me, and together, we made primeval sounds in the dark, little grunts. So this was what it was like, this was what all the fuss was about. This, this, what is this? It tastes very good. Mmmh.

'Gerroff,' said Kath.

I gorroff doing that, and gorron with the business in hand, foot, loins, mouth and arms. It was a truly magnificent evening. Afterwards we lay in each others arms with our feet protruding from the duvet and we slept like logs.

22

The following morning, I woke early and waded down through the rubble of prostrate and supine glue sniffers sleeping or comatose on the floorplanks. The kitchen was in the same position as it had been the night before. This was a surprise. The kettle wasn't and nor were the windows; they had disappeared. I was feeling altogether very happy and pleased. I went up to the roof, picked up my helmet from its hiding place, went back down, and outside, started my motor-cycle. I rode in the sun with the blue sky and no traffic. In Hammersmith, I found a café. I bought two teas and two bacon sandwiches and took them back to the squat. And she was still sleeping in the morning sunlight.

I drank my tea looking at Kath. Kath and all Kath, under the duvet Kath, white-haired, sleeping and lips parted Kath. I woke her.

'I brought you tea and a sandwich,' I said sitting next to her on the mattress. Then I remembered the flowers and got up and went up on the roof to fetch them but when I found them they had no heads. I brought them down anyway and told Kath about them and she kissed me and said I was sweet and then Chopper came in and as soon as he saw the flowers he said, 'Look what Daisy done,' and shook his head.

'Did he do this?' I asked.

'Afraid so,' said Chopper. 'Can't leave any flowers around when he's drunk. He'll eat the lot.'

I was sad about that but there wasn't anything that

would make me go and have words with him for he was one big bastard. A monster, even.

'Don't worry, James,' said Kath. 'It was a nice thought, thank you.'

Her saying that sort of made it not matter and she gave me another kiss and then it didn't matter.

'I reckon we should go to Margate today,' said Chopper looking up at the sky. 'It'd be a good ride. You want to go?'

'Yes!' Kath squealed.

'Of course,' said I. 'When?'

'After breakfast.'

It was then that we heard drum beats – wild, mad erratic ones coming from downstairs.

'What's that?' said Kath.

'Either Norman's blocked the toilet again,' said Chopper, 'or it's Rita lamenting Daisy's departure.'

'Where did he go?' I asked.

'His wife came late last night and fought with Rita over Daisy. It was a hell of a fight, swearing and biting and pulling and scratching. I wouldn't have fought either of them. They were a bunch of savages. You should have been there. Best fight I've seen this year. Magic.'

'Who won?' Kath asked.

'The other girl knocked Rita out with a lovely right cross – put her out cold. And by the time Rita came to, Daisy had been carted off. Did old Rita scream! Cor, deafening it was.'

Then Sherry walked in and told Chopper she was hungry and wanted breakfast so they went off to find some.

We left the house about eleven and headed off in the sun with Rita at the front and Frank bringing up the rear. The roads were awful crowded with the traffic that appears only at the weekends when the sun is out. There were cars towing boats and cars with caravans and cars that were just stuffed full of people and when we sped

186

past cars with children, they would always wave and smile.

We rode through South London on the South Circular and joined the A2 at Greenwich and there we stopped briefly for petrol at an old Esso station. When we climbed back onto the road we were joined by other men on touring machines and further on, after Dartford, we rode up on a band of Angels. We didn't stay with them though because they rode too slow and soon we were running in top, in a long snaking line in the fast lane of the M2 coming down the shallow run to the bridge at Roche. Here, a bank of fog hung whilst the sun shone everywhere else. Just on the bridge. On our side and on the other side, there was not a cloud to be seen. We rode into the white and the cars were slowing in the other lanes as we thundered through at eighty.

On the other side, as we climbed away from the bridge, we rode into sunlight. The road sliced the face of a hill and the countryside opened up; below, in the green fields, there were islands of tall pines on the small rolling hills, and behind, where the sky and the hills met, there were clouds. Chopper was ahead now as we stormed the countryside, riding on the good roads. These were certainly fine roads, I was thinking.

The road was well surfaced and made of good concrete that provided traction for the hot-and-melting rubber as we swooped through fast curves running on the inside or the outside of the lane, but not on the middle, not on the chocolate black, exhaust-streaked middle line. There, with the motor-cycle laid over in a fast curve, it feels all wrong and you are always waiting for the front end to go.

We were making very good time. We had travelled to Roche in forty-five minutes from the squat and soon we were to be off the motorway riding on a two-laned A road. The road looked wonderful ahead, but most of the cars were stacked up behind a slow-moving dump truck that was making a lot of smoke. Here the country was flat and green and some of the fields were furrowed, and all the time there were pylons and power lines criss-crossing it all and wrecking the good looking land. The cars were taking a long time to peel off from behind the dump truck and pass it. We rode alongside them all, passing them and the dump truck, and leaving them to gain an open road. We came to a section that looked perfect to work and when we got nearer we all knew it was going to be good and we wound it on. The section ran downhill in a series of long, sweeping, cut-back turns, with the camber of the turn running with the bend, and we went streaming down the hill in single file letting Frank go first on the wide-cylindered BMW that looked, from behind, to be sloppy in its handling. Then there was Norman, and his motor-cycle was struggling to keep up. Kath and I rode in the middle of all of them with her holding on around my midriff, and her head on my shoulder looking forward at the way the road ran. This section of road was all about rhythm and the right line. Sometimes, when your judgement was off, the rhythm would be ruined and you'd be all over the brakes and it would take time to get back in the flow. I made a mistake about halfway down and Chopper came through on the outside, running blind, on a left-hander.

At the bottom, the road flattened out for a while and then climbed up slowly, with cabbage fields on either side, smelling rotten. Frank and Chopper were playing up ahead, both of them running hard. We passed a 'Snacks' coach parked in a lay-by; the side was opened up ready for service. Then we came to a small round-about where Frank and Chopper had waited for us. This was near Greenhill. In twenty minutes, we were riding down the hill onto the sea-front at Margate.

'Oh look,' Kath said. 'I'nne lovely?'

A black mongrel dog was jumping high off the sand to reach a stick held by his owner, a man. The beach was crowded and we parked the motor-cycles in front of one of the many arcades that lined the front.

'What d'you want to do?' Chopper said.

'I want a pint,' said Rita.

We walked along the front and cut through a small back street and on this street we found a pub. It was a small and smoky room populated by large overweight men, their wives and their children. In the middle of the room, strategically placed in order to ensure the maximum amount of discomfort to the pub's drinkers, there was an old, well-worn pool table. Here, two giants at the game battled, potted, smoked, spat, and swore their way through an epic marathon that lasted the duration of our two drinks apiece. When we left the pub, only two balls had been sunk.

On the front, we sought the fun fair as a source of potential amusement. We paid our entrance fee to a wizened old bag, who sat in a booth reading, and joined the mass of people already inside, to wait in line for a ride on the ferris wheel. I was allowed to place my arm around the slender, bare shoulders of the creamily skinned Kath. The fingers were allowed to drape only as far as the collar-bone; any further explorative wanderings were rewarded with a sharp thwack across the knuckles. Sometimes she would add, 'You filthy bugger!' and giggled.

I was not wishing to be a filthy bugger, of course, I only wanted the innocent thrill of discovery as Kath had everything of everything that I had ever dreamt of in my early youth and, indeed, everything and all that an admirer of beauty could wish for. At least, that is how I thought of her.

On the ferris wheel we sat and our legs touched as I held grimly onto the side of the small carriage as she rocked the bugger ferociously in a seemingly suicidal bid to accomplish the not so impossible feat of turning the box seat upside down, and sending us to our doom on the concrete below. Around and around we went with Kath screaming profane slogans of encouragement for me to work harder in her quest for the ultimate thrill. And all the time, I, like a stupid bastard, grinned, gripped and pretended to oblige her.

At the end of the ride, we were freed from this hideous contraption by an evil-smirking, ruddy-faced youth who obviously appreciated the everything and all in a creature of beauty and followed my precious with his eyes, as we all walked away from the wheel, with me gently rubbing my abdomen.

They were all completely unmanageable in their enthusiasm for pursuing their quest for fun. To me it seemed that the only likely outcome of such behaviour was a stomach wrenching conversation with the loo. I tried, in vain, to persuade them that games played on the beach could be of equal enjoyment; but such suggestions were only met with derision. I was still making feeble pleas when the bar was secured around my waist, the bell rang and the music started.

Kath squealed with delight.

The machine that we sat in was known as the 'Octopus'. This was because it had many tentacles, steel ones, and in place of suckers it had us sitting in small booths. Once started, we were hurled from one side of the octopus's lair to the other, missing all the other suckers travelling in the opposite direction by inches. It would have been a charming ride but for the speed at which we travelled. The booth could, I was sure, out-accelerate any motor-cycle found anywhere. I felt like a fish might feel when it was being slapped up against the wall of the lair, in preparation for dinner for Mr Octopus. The only difference being that the wall I was slapped against was nice and soft, and sat next to me.

'Isn't this great!' Kath said.

I couldn't answer. I wanted to and undoubtedly what I

would have said would have been a filthy lie but as I said, I physically couldn't. I was sick. My stomach and I were involved in a terrible struggle. It was a question of mind over matter, and matter was winning.

Luckily, twenty pence won't buy you much. It bought us approximately three minutes and just at the moment where I thought it was all over for me, and I'd have to let it all out, it was all over.

'Wot a con!' moaned Kath.

Wot a miracle, I thought, and smiled feebly in her direction. We were swarmed by little kids as we climbed out.

''ere mister,' said one waiting for me to lift my shaking frame. 'Can't you 'urry up?'

'What's the rush?' I said.

''im,' said the little kid pointing to an equally scruffy little boy hovering behind. I got out quickly and the little kid dived into my seat and slapped down the bar.

'How 'bout the dive bomber, then?' said Chopper as we stood watching the octopus thrill a fresh selection of screaming kids and adults. I made no reply. Everybody else was extremely enthusiastic.

'All right,' said Rita. 'But first let's get some food. I'm hungry.'

'Candy floss!' Norman shouted.

'And hot dogs with ketchup!' said Frank.

'I want a beer,' said Chopper.

We walked through the crowded fair-ground in the afternoon sun. Kath was ahead, talking to Sherry. Chopper and Frank were behind and they were involved in an animated discussion on crowd control techniques applied by the police at football matches. Norman was wandering nearby looking at all the different colours of the fair stalls and I was scheming at the rear.

How am I going to get out of this? I thought. Walk away, that's one way. Or maybe lag so far behind that

you lose them and when they've finished punishing themselves, they will come and find you, all broken hearted
about not being able to share with them in such maso-
chistic pleasures, sitting on your motor-cycle. You could
do that, certainly you could do that. I was going to do
that, in fact I was doing it, lagging behind and searching
for a small crowded passageway to blend into, when
Chopper dropped back to talk to me. We talked boys'
talk and all the time I was trying to discover a solution to
an insoluble problem.

Backing down and declining to ride in this creature
they called the dive bomber would be a lousy loss of face
and I doubted if Kath would have approved. She was like
that. She liked everything tough.

'Chopper, where did the ape Johnny go?'

'Dunno. He went home I think.'

'Did you see him before he went?'

'Yeah. He wanted to know where you were, he said he
had something for you. Wanted to know where you
lived. Said it was important.'

'Did you tell him?'

'Nah.'

'Thanks.'

Anyway, this thing they call the dive bomber, it can't
be any worse than any of the others. It was probably
better. It had to be. I know what it is, I thought. I have
seen kids playing on them. It's a little aeroplane that goes
round and round and up and down. You can handle that,
certainly you can. It might even be a pleasure.

We bought candy floss. Frank ate a couple of hotdogs.
Chopper drank his beer, and Kath was uncontrollably
excited and wished us all to hurry up. She was more
excited than a little child at Christmas.

By now I was feeling quite enthusiastic. The dive
bomber was sure to be a pleasure. Now, I could contribute to the conversation with almost equal amounts of

enthusiasm as the others. That was, of course, until I saw it.

It was on the other side of the fair-ground. Kath pointed to it and shrieked, 'There it is! Look at it!' It was a hideous sight. Like two giant revolving suppositories fixed at opposite ends of a forty-foot arm. Not only did these foul looking things spin round on a vertical axis, they also spin laterally.

'Is that the dive bomber?' I said.

'Yeah,' said Kath. 'Isn't it great!'

Run!

That was the first thing I thought of doing. It turned out to be the only thing I thought of doing and when I did it, I was caught.

'Where're you goin'?' said Kath.

'I don't know,' I said truthfully.

'Are you chicken?'

'Nope,' I lied. I was terrified. Not only did this scare me, but just the sight of the beast made me want to throw up, violently. Perhaps it would be better for all if you came clean with her right now, before it was too late. But I didn't.

We queued and we were packed, carefully, into our suppositories. I kept quiet. I kept my fingers crossed. I kept my mouth shut and my jaw locked. We started. The ride only cost twenty pence. A good omen, I thought.

At the highest point of the circle we stopped. Ha! It was over. Wrong. They were filling the other capsule.

'C'mon!' Kath shouted out the side, impatiently.

'All right luv,' came a voice from below. 'Hold your horses.'

This was going to be worse than death itself. I tried to hold the hand of my love under the pretext that I was soothing away whatever fears she might have held. She said, 'Are you scared or something?' I smiled and braced my feet against the front, and gripped the harness.

As it turned out the ride wasn't so bad. I threw up but I knew that was going to happen, it was simply a matter of time. Fortunately for Kath and myself, and anyone standing in a radius of fifty feet from the revolving, twirling dive bomber, it happened afterwards. Kath was disgusted and utterly ashamed of my weak stomach. She wouldn't talk to me. Chopper thought it all highly amusing and mocked me mercilessly all the way out of the fair and onto the sand of the beach.

I did a bit of sulking then and went down to the beach and scuffed my shoes in the sand and threw stones and walked about all mad whilst the others went and joined in a game of football. I was pretty good at sulking and when I was finally finished with it I went and sat on a bench up top on the road, not down on the beach. The beach was crowded full of these funny people that sat in their deckchairs with their bellies hanging out of their shirts and their sandals on their naked toes, and on their heads they wore their handkerchiefs with a knot in each corner to make them smaller and a good fit. They sat down there sunning themselves and every now and then the dad would raise himself out of his chair to have a stretch and a look around. When he was satisfied that everything was how it should be he'd sit himself back down and would go dozing. Then the mum would get a little curious and once the dad was asleep she'd place down the knitting and she'd get up and have a look about. Then she'd sit right down again. Ay, funny game, cricket.

Sometimes a couple of fellows on motor-cycles would come haring down the seafront on their dinky little Fizzy's all kitted up with expansion chambers. You could hear them when they were miles away and nowhere to be seen. I'd watch them come from either end of the front as they swooped down the hill, running abreast and in file, and they'd ride along the front all slow – just checking to see what was there and was worth looking at. Then they'd sort of get bored of that and they'd park their motor-cycles in front of the arcades that lined the length of the seafront, and get off, really slow and saddle sore, and then they'd mosey on in, after a quick look about to make sure all the little ladies around were watching.

Then there were others on the front who had big machines and loafed on them. These boys were a pretty hairy bunch that liked their leather and denim and loved talking bike. Well, if the truth be known it was mostly sex but they did an awful lot of pointing and crawling about on the road examining the machines.

When I'd finished looking at how things were in this place I turned back and looked at Kath playing on the beach with all these skinheads who were performing for her like dogs in a circus. They were meant to be playing football but it didn't seem to me as if the ball made any difference to the game they were playing and they could have probably played without it. You see the only thing these men were doing was flattening each other and yelling and stomping a lot. This game went on for quite some time and a lot of the lesser men had to retire hurt and when they did, Kath would poke fun at them and tease them. Finally Chopper said the game was over and after much grunting the game was disbanded and the skinheads went off, shouting and chanting and causing a nuisance. We mounted up and left, though Kath still wasn't too pleased with me.

Frank led with Rita, and Chopper and myself followed and Norman brought up the rear. We rode out and when we went I could feel the eyes of the men with the big machines, watching. It was about five now and a lot of cars were leaving with us and so as we went up the hill that climbed away and left the sea to the right, we stayed in the middle of the road passing them.

A few miles on and the traffic was running a little better and soon we were riding the good roads where you could open her up and storm by. And now the wind blew, warm and refreshing and I had my visor up and my jacket open and I was enjoying myself. When we came to roundabouts – and there were quite a few in this flat land – you could take four to five cars on the braking into; a couple on the way round; and a couple on the way out – depending how close they were. This was always fine because you could stuff the bike right down into the turn so that the footpegs would lick up the concrete and wind the power on hard so the front would go a little light as the back started to break away. We were riding this way and were enjoying ourselves in this relaxing manner when all of a sudden these three motor-cycles came screaming past on the inside and the outside of me as I was leisurely carving a line through some slow and stubborn caravans.

They were riding big machines – I reckoned one was a CB900F, the other was a Gs750 and the other one looked like a Gs1000 but I wasn't sure because a lot of those big machines have a similar tail section. So Kath reacted almost instantaneously in a manner that any genius would have predicted.

'Go on!' she screamed at my helmeted ear, and for the first time in an afternoon barren from physical contact, she touched me. Admittedly it was not a silken caress, but a full-blooded thump in between the shoulders. '*Catch 'em!*'

They were closing on Chopper when he saw them and put it down a gear in the box. They did not catch him. We followed hard, with the Lc screaming at the red line before each upshift. My ten thousand mile motor wanted to rev and over rev with its two passengers smothered in an ungamely aerodynamic position, lying prone on the fuel tank, out of the winds reach.

Here was the chance to redeem myself, I was thinking. Her arms no longer ignored my little belly. The closer I came to disaster, the more she would tighten her grip. Kath worked my midriff like a jockey riding a racehorse with a soft mouth and sensitive flanks. And behaving like any horse would under the circumstances, with her firm fleshy breasts digging at my shoulders, I gunned the motor and rode that road with the devil, and the clocks showing just the other side of a hundred.

We ran enormous risks chasing down the five that were ahead. Under normal circumstances, there would not have been a competition as such. A small chase, perhaps. But no competition. The capacities of the motors of the machines they rode would have ridiculed any such suggestion. It was in our favour that they were unaware of the circumstances behind, and causing the revolt in my right fist, my throttle hand. Nothing could have stopped me; the evil and foul-smelling memories of those five minutes spent vomiting behind the beer tent, and the tortuous afternoon lying in solitude and misery whilst my firm breasted lovely revealed a little too much flesh during an over enthusiastic game of football with a band of filthy mouthed skinheads, corrupted any sense of reason, and cocked the throttle to the stop.

One hundred and ten miles an hour.

I stormed the roads and the flimsy dress worn by my love, beat at my legs in an urgent rhythm. The drivers of the cars in the oncoming lane beat at their horns, as we bore down on them, headlight flashing warning signals to those who dared to run at us head-on. They pulled out of the way as we scorched past, cursing us as we went. We were up on the tail ender now. We were over in a righthander and the bike was shaking us as the front end started to buck. I knocked it back and felt a gut wrenching squeeze from my jockey companion. I wound it back

197

on, and it shook until the road straightened itself. We passed the first of the four, about three inches from the dirt and disaster, running past him on the inside. He was not expecting such a manoeuvre and before he had a chance to parry our move, I sliced him up, going in front of him and taking his line for the next car and the next bend. He rode a red seven fifty Suzuki.

My stomach was caressed with encouragement. I felt her look away from my shoulder at the man we had passed, she might have made a mocking gesture with her hand, I'm not sure, but I felt one of her hands leave my stomach and then return. The others were not so far ahead, now. A hundred yards only.

We were riding through open land and the rotting smell of cabbages filled the helmet that I wore in the dusk that was settling. We caught them as they waited for a line of juggernauts to clear the opposite lane and allow passage in front of a garbage truck that held them up. It sat wide and slow and smoking. Seeing the opportunity here to impress shock and frighten the girl that seemed to derive a mad and insatiable pleasure from such feelings as fear, I slowed the machine until we were running at over eighty and pointed it to the inside of the garbage truck, to the three-foot strip of black tarmac walled by rolling steel and black rubber on one side and dirt on the other. The others were still locked in single file waiting for the road to clear as we slipped by. Kath waved to them.

The truck driver, no doubt about it, was a bastard. Half-way through, and the truck moves in on us. I had to move onto the dirt until we were in front. Fortunately, the motor-cycle kept a straight line and kept upright. I don't think I breathed once. Still, my pouting lovely urged me to go faster. I was up on the road again and running flat out and the road was clear of cars. The garbage man hooted indignantly.

It was then that I started to think like a sane person. We had distance on the others, as the convoy of artics coming the other way was followed immediately by an army convoy out on manoeuvres. What the hell was I going to do? If I was to turn off the road and pretend to get lost somewhere she would still insist that I drove like a maniac. To her, this business of racing had taken paramount importance, above life and limb. Her twisted mind grabbed hold of danger like old Jack would attack a rat, shaking it by the neck until it was dead. Ten miles down the road and I didn't have to worry any more. We had run out of petrol. I brought the motor-cycle to rest and Yorkletts was three miles away.

She was not happy about this development. Kath dismounted and stood away from the motor-cycle, by the roadside, all disgusted, and watched the traffic and waited for sign of the others. I had just removed my helmet when I heard the tuned rumbling sound of the four-cylindered 860 Honda. They came past with Chopper running in front. I put my thumb out and they didn't stop.

'Go on, Chopper!' screamed my sulking lovely as they thundered away in the direction of the hill that had given us much pleasure earlier in the day. They were riding into the sun that rested itself like a large sunburnt head on great green shoulders.

Other traffic piled past and when it was the turn of the garbage truck, he hooted and one of the men in the cab flashed a 'V' sign out the window.

'Why d'you have to run out of petrol?' little Kath demanded, her face red with anger.

'It was an accident,' I said.

'Why didn't you fill up earlier?'

'I would have at Herne Bay, but you wouldn't let me.'

'You're a wanker,' she said.

When I lifted the petrol cap and looked inside, I saw fuel.

'What did you say?' I said knowing full well what she had said but wanting to make sure in any case.

'You're a wanker,' she said once more. I switched the fuel tap to the 'reserve' position and let the fuel run to the carbs. This was a tricky one to deal with and having nothing up my sleeve to answer such allegations, I flicked the kick-start out from its resting position by the side-panel, and in two kicks the engine was ticking away on idle. Kath was still standing by the roadside.

'How come it's working?' she said.

I told her that it must have been a blockage in one of the pipes, that we were indeed very lucky to be alive as such blockages have been known in the past to seize motors solid and send the riders of such machines sliding down the road on their backsides. Kath failed to see the dangerous aspect of such lies and instead chose to focus her attention on the more pressing matter of who would have paid the cost of a new dress if such an accident had occurred. Obviously in her mind she was quite satisfied that dying was something that was only accomplished on a regular basis by people of old age. Having convinced her that the motor-cycle was now safe to ride and that we wouldn't ride fast (in case this mysterious blockage should again occur and have more disastrous consequences), we set off. I wondered how far it was to the nearest petrol station as the reserve part of the tank had a capacity for I wasn't sure how much and I doubted if the same story would have worked twice. I rode at a leisurely pace changing up at five grand and trying to conserve petrol. It was not long before Rita and Norman were riding with us.

Unfortunately, Yorkletts – a town that I had put much hope in – had no open petrol stations. Having tricked

Kath into believing something disastrous could happen imminently, she held my midriff reluctantly. We found petrol at a station on the side of the road just before we joined the M2.

23

Had I known what I was to expect on arrival at the squat, I should have left my dear sweet Kath standing on the roadside three miles from Yorkletts, cursing me, my motorcycle, and the filthy Sherry for having made her ride home with me.

I recognised the bikes parked outside the squat, alongside the cow-horned 860, as belonging to those whom we had raced on the road from Margate. Why they were here was a complete mystery and one that would only be resolved by entering the squat. Of course, the first question they asked as we walked in the room, was an embarrassing one.

'Couldn't find the reserve, could ya?' said Chopper in between sips of a can of Fosters. I decided that the best response to a potentially damaging question was a red herring.

'How did you manage to get back so quickly? When did you arrive?'

'Twenty minutes ago.'

'He said we could have seized,' said Kath. 'Otherwise we would have beaten you.'

Perhaps she smelt a fish, I was thinking. A large red one. Chopper grinned and said, 'He said what?'

You must move the conversation and quickly, I thought. I didn't, and Kath repeated herself. Old Chopper thought this highly amusing and burst into laughter, his extra-strong, extra-large booties twitching with delight.

'Don't laugh at me!' Kath snapped.

'Didn't ya?' said Kath.

Somehow I skirted disaster and managed to weave a tale of lies that, by the end, convinced even myself of the veracity of such nonsense. I made references to dangerous readings on the temperature gauge, a suspected rupture in one of the radiator hoses, etc, etc.

'Oh yeah,' said Chopper not believing a single word of anything I had said or could say. He had the smile of a mischievous schoolboy as he looked at me and I think he must have seen something in my face, perhaps the simple and often gratifying sight of a mirrored reflection of a kindred soul, that prevented him from continuing the cross-examination. Instead he said, 'Norman, go get some beer.'

'Why should I go?' said Norman.

'I thought you'd like to go. Daisy said he'd be round any minute and that was fifteen minutes ago . . .'

Chopper had not even finished his sentence when we heard the door close and Norman mount his aged beast, and in no time at all he was away and heading for the off-licence.

Now we were all introduced. There was Tom, sitting in the wretched and burnt carcass of an armchair (a victim of some pagan ritual carried out in the early hours of the morning) – owner of the red 750 Suzuki.

'Hallo Tom,' I said.

No reply.

The other three sat on the couch in their black leather jackets, round shouldered, spindly limbed, long haired and dirty faced. There was not an inch on these lads that had not been claimed by some form of slogan. It was written, sown and painted into every well-worn and dirty piece of denim or leather worn by the three. Sex seemed to be the predominant theme and music a close second. They had gormless expressions on their faces and not much to say for themselves. The conversation, which was more like a multiple choice question and answer sheet, soon found its way to the only common denominator that could be shared amongst the occupants of the room. Motor-cycles, motors, leathers, racers and finally after a few joints had been smoked and a few grateful cans downed (bought by the returned Norman) it got down to a good bit of bragging.

We all bragged about everything. But mostly we bragged about motor-cycles and here is where the trouble started. What with the presence of Kath, and the knowledge that she was highy impressed and captivated by this thing with danger, I set about bragging with an unusual amount of verve and inspiration. For a while I was a genius at this bragging game, silencing the mutes on the couch with thundering explosions of self-inflating loquacious talk, leaving them squashed on the road-side, like a pigeon or pussy-cat, as I surged ahead accumulating more stories per mile and more points per second in the eyes of my beloved. I think she was genuinely entranced by my performance. But then, disaster struck.

Tom spoke.

'If you're so great,' said the quiet force that sat calmly, surveying this harmless scene of loud-mouthed camaraderie, 'prove it.'

Tom had a weasel's face, that much I had noticed before. Now, stunned into silence and staring him right between the eyes I thought I could detect a small twinkle in those empty orbs, a faint smile on his lips. He had something in store for me. His nose twitched. All eyes were focused on mine. I felt a trembling in the bowels.

'How?' I said.

'A race,' said Tom, his lips breaking open to reveal a crooked smile.

'We haven't got equal machinery,' said I watching him survey Kath. The dirty bugger, I thought. He had speculated quite rightly on what it was that appealed to her nature. We were to duel and she was to be the prize. Back to the Wild West. The Knights even, and all that rubbish. Was I willing to take him up on this sneaky and conniving challenge? Of course. The tender succulent memories of a night spent in her sweet embrace, and the lonely months preceding such activity, necessitated a firm and fearless stance.

'What's the prize?' said Kath coyly.

Aha! So she was fishing now. Tom looked at her. Kath looked at him. They looked at me.

'I don't know,' I said. 'You tell me.'

And so he did.

'Your bird,' he said.

'My what?' I said.

'Your bird.'

'She isn't my bird, and if she was, she wouldn't be mine to give away. She belongs to herself, not to me. I can't put her up.'

That was what I thought a person adopting a firm and fearless stance should say. Something noble, chivalrous and up to date with the current trends. Well, that was the wrong thing to say. Kath didn't like it. In fact, she hated me for it.

Kath left the room. I had not a clue what I had done wrong. Chopper shook his head.

'She doesn't approve,' I said.

'All right. I'll race you for your bike.'

'Yeah, go on Jimmy. Have him,' said Chopper, now standing in the middle of the room, smiling.

'Are you stupid?' I asked. 'How's my little Lc going to come near that big brute of a motor-cycle you ride?'

I was looking for a way out. Kath was no longer in the room. She would not disown me if she couldn't hear what was being said. But old Chopper – he was a little bit too keen for my liking. He had ideas, I thought. A bad sign.

'You don't have to race on the Lc,' said Tom.

'What else am I going to race on?' said I.

'Not my problem.'

'Go on, James,' said Rita getting up from the sofa and knocking over a couple of tins in the process. 'You can have him.'

But I didn't want him. I didn't want to race. All I wanted was Kath. Now, I had a nasty suspicion that squat pride was at stake. And I, the most successful bragger in the building, had, in effect, talked my way into the position of Defender Of The Faith. Chopper confirmed the appointment by saying, 'Don't worry about it, James. I can sort something out for you.'

At that moment I could have sworn I heard the rusted and unoiled hinges of a coffin lid closing. But it wasn't – it was Daisy in his leather trousers.

24

I did not get to sleep with Kath that evening. Or the following night or even the whole of the next week. She didn't want to see me. My heart was broken, I think.

When I went into the cafe, she ignored me. My bacon and eggs were served by the lovely Vera's wrinkled hands. When I tried to talk to her, she'd turn her back on me and rush into the kitchen saying, 'Order in! Order in!'

I waited for her, in ambush, outside the cafe. But each attempt was foiled at lunch-time by Vera. Kath was not allowed out until all the customers had left and the lunch-hour was officially over. By which time old Stanley had got me working. In the evenings, when I returned to the office after the work had been completed, the 'Closed' sign would be hanging in the darkened windows of the cafe and there would be no sign of her. Miserable and dejected. I would go back to the squat and bury my sorrows under my duvet with only my pillow for comfort. I slept a lot in that week. By Friday, I had decided that if she was not going to see me, I must see her. Pook had told me this.

For the race, I had not paid much attention. It was of secondary consideration. It was to be held on a section of the North Circular, between Wembley and Brent Cross. Chopper had made the arrangements. We were to race at four o'clock on Sunday morning, in two weeks' time. I didn't know what I was to ride and I didn't care. I was pining for my mate.

Friday evening. I could not bear to be separated from

her any longer. I rode to Hackney. I schemed many things. Memorised many speeches; none of them mine. I cribbed them from famous romantic ones made in the past. I fiddled with them, changing the names, adding bits, modernising them. They sounded terrible. I hid behind her tower block, in wait. Where was she?

She was out, and what was worse was that she was with him – the strangler Johnny. I watched them walk across the courtyard together, arm in arm. Enraged, and drunk with jealousy, I kicked the motor-cycle into life and charged at them. I would have killed them if they hadn't split up and ran for cover. I was sure of it.

Having missed on the first attempt, I slid the motor-cycle at the far end of the courtyard, next to John Ruskin House, and made a second lightning pass. The glue sniffer Johnny took to his heels and fled from the courtyard, running faster than any jackrabbit I have ever seen. Those extra-strong, extra-large booties lapped up the concrete at a most encouraging rate. I watched him happily, as he ran off, skirting the concrete playground opposite, under the yellow light from the streetlamps. I was grinning.

'You coward!' screamed my breathless Kath standing on the first landing of Aberfeldy House and leaning out of the window. She was screaming at the glue sniffer. She had not recognised my machine. I took my helmet off turned off the headlight. Now, she could see me.

'Bastard!' she screamed. 'How dare you do a thing like that? You should be . . .'

She swore at me for nearly a full five minutes. It was magnificent. I was happy. She was talking to me after a week in the wilderness.

When she had finished, she slammed the landing window and disappeared. I dismounted and quickly went inside. The elevators in the building did not work. I had to walk to the fifteenth floor.

'She don't want to see you,' said her father.

Out of breath, I begged with him. I pleaded with him. I made all sorts of promises I couldn't keep, but still the answer remained the same. 'Bugger off.'

Downstairs, I sat in the middle of the courtyard on my motor-cycle, in the dark. A few couples drifted in and out of the buildings surrounding the courtyard. Lovers cooing in each others ears. I brooded.

Then, I had an idea. A good one it was too. I started the motor-cycle. I revved the engine deliberately, and kept doing so until residents of the surrounding blocks leaned out of their windows and made all sorts of malicious threats to my person. Finally, Kath peered out from the fifteenth floor. It was then that I snuck the bike into gear.

I made a rubber painting.

It was a variation on a trick we used to practise on dirt bikes: spinning doughnuts. Only this doughnut was heart-shaped. A beautiful fifteen-foot wide burnt-rubber heart. Made with the rear type spinning and the front brake on.

It worked. I was applauded by the residents and visited by Kath. When we talked I discovered I had been standing on the wrong foot when I was making my firm and fearless stance. Not only was I on the wrong foot, I learnt that I had completely misunderstood her motives for refusing to see me.

Kath was sulking. I had insulted her by refusing to make her the prize. It was ludicrous, but it was true. I promised to make amends.

25

I should tell you a little, now, about the process behind the choice of machine for this epic duel to be fought on the blacktop; about the method applied to attain such a machine; and, indeed, why old Chopper would go to such lengths to procure a speedy foil for my use. But I can't. If I did, it might be used as incriminating evidence, in a forthcoming court-case.

I have a man, a detective from the criminal investigation squad at Wembley, I think his name is Proby, who comes and visits me here at the hospital. He thinks I was riding a stolen motor-cycle when I had my accident. Of course, I had to tell him the truth: of the journey home from Hackney in the early hours of that fateful Sunday morning; of me, riding with a broken heart (snapped in the malicious hands of my lovely); of a dog stepping out from the kerb and into the speeding path of my motor-cycle; of the ensuing rubber-tearing slide and bone-breaking fall caused not only by the pooch's ignorance of the green cross code, but also by my lack of attention until it was all too late. Admittedly, I was travelling a little faster than the speed limit permitted (this remark was scoffed at by the cruel and cold-eyed Proby who quoted a distance of some eighty feet as the length of the burnt rubber skid-mark found at the scene of the accident), and if the crime was a crime, it had to be excused, or the severity of the crime reduced, on the grounds that it was a crime passionel. (This, Proby found highly amusing and would have choked had the nurse not been stupid enough to bring him a glass of water.)

Where was the bike? I had no idea. Somebody must have stolen it, I said. After all, by the time the police were notified that an accident had occured on the North Circular it was six hours later, whilst I was lying in a semi-conscious stupor in the emergency ward at Saint Marcus's Hospital, Wembley. (Again, more scoffing from Detective Proby.)

And the dog? There was no sign of a broken and mangled mutt. Well there wouldn't be, I said, because I missed it. That was why I skidded and fell.

When Detective Proby asked me who the skinhead was that brought me to the hospital in a van and why it was that he did not stay long enough for his name to be taken, I could only reply that I was unconscious at the time and remembered and saw nothing until I woke an hour later on the operating table. I assumed he must have been passing by after the accident occurred, saw me lying on the roadside next to my broken machine, rushed me to hospital and perhaps returned to take the motor-cycle. Who knows? I certainly didn't.

For some strange reason, Proby didn't believe me. He thought, and it was a ridiculous thought, that I had been street-racing. He has made at least five trips up to the ward (the bastard never brings me flowers) and each visit seems no different from the time before. The same questions are asked whilst I piddle in my bed pan and scratch my rotting kneecaps with a coat-hanger. I don't know how much longer he's going to pester me but I have a feeling that it will all sort itself out in the end. (I'm not sure how expensive this feeling is.)

I have other feelings, too. We have this beaut of a nurse on the ward, called Fiona. She changes my dressings; she looks after me; I think I love her. Last night, the hospital had an anniversary party, a sort of dance thing. We were the best couple there. I had the two-wheeled Rumba down to a tee. I never ran over her toes once in the grey-backed wheelchair I had been loaned. I was a champion at it. Wheelies, doughnuts, power slides – I could do them all. I had to be the best show-off in the hall.

Then, when I was being lowered into my cot after the dance had finished, I had a thought. As thoughts go, it was quite a big one and it kept me awake most of the night. It concerns women. It's pretty sad. The thing is this: if you look at History right the way back to the Bible, men are always doing stupid and idiotic acts in order to impress women. I had a teacher once, Mr Doggart, who knew all these great things about history, and one afternoon he told us a story of Bluebeard the Pirate. He said old Bluebeard slaughtered each of his many wives, it might have been only most of them, in order to impress the next one up. He was that mad about them. What is sad is that I know why the man did it. If I'd been him, I'll bet I'd have done the same if the woman had wanted it. This thought, being enormous and grossly significant at the time, needed immediate airing in conversation. But it being late at night and the ward being full of sleeping Pakistanis, I had no option other to wake the drunken and dozing Scotsman that lay in the bed next to mine. His name was Angus. He had broken an arm and a leg when he fell off a bar stool singing in the Hope & Anchor. I'd seen him in jail, I'd watched him on television and now I wanted to talk to him. But the bastard wouldn't wake, he would only snore. Instead, I tinkled quietly and with great restraint into my bedpan and listened in the dark to the sound of little pennies dropping on a tin floor.

Today, they all visited me. I had my friends from the squat and my family all in the same room at the same time. But they stood on either side of an invisible line that divided the bed into two. My mother and father didn't even acknowledge that Rita and the boys were standing in the same room, let alone talking to the same patient.

'I've brought you some food, dear,' Mother said to me

as Rita was explaining the fickle nature of Kath's affections. (Both conversations being conducted simultaneously.) 'I thought you'd like some rock cakes for your tea.' Mother smiled and I smiled at her, trying not to be rude to Rita who had carried on regardless.

For a moment I thought all was well and that we had come to an unspoken understanding, where certain things would be best left unmentioned. The rock cakes were a peace offering and one that would be taken gratefully, though consumed reluctantly. The very act of consumption should have been a hint of what was to follow.

''ere,' said Chopper. 'When you fuckin' gettin' out of 'ere?' Chopper lounged in an armchair with his boots on my bed.

Pook finished adding his initials to a small virgin piece of grubby white plaster (somewhere just above the right ankle) and looked at Mother. She acted as if nothing had been said though we both knew that such talk was highly offensive to her. I watched Pook close his eyes.

'I don't know,' I said.

'Stanley wants to know when you're goin' to be back.'

'You aren't going back, James,' Mother said.

My father continued, 'We have found a school that will accept you, James. It's not a bad little school. It's in Devon actually. They're the only school we could find that would give you a place. You start September the fifth.' Dad coughed.

'Yeah,' said Chopper ignoring my dad. 'Stanley's got a load more clients now, Jimmy. There's a fortune to be had. I told him I thought you'd be ready by then. You are comin' back incha?'

'You're not, James,' said Mum.

'What d'you mean he ain't? Let him make up his own mind. What you goin' to do, Jimmy?'

'I don't know.'

Now Mother talked to me. She said I must not go back.

Then Dad, then Chopper, then all of them together and none of them listened. I didn't know. I still don't. I pulled up the bed sheets. They still talked, but now without me. Then there was a whole lot of arguing, then some shouting and then they left. When they had gone and all was quiet, I slept. I dreamt of pirates.

The boys are back together again!

AUF WIEDERSEHEN *Pet.*
TWO

by Fred Taylor

Now available: the second novel based on the hugely popular
series by Dick Clement and Ian La Frenais, probably the best
script-writing team in Britain today.

In response to an SOS from Barry, our heroes reassemble –
more than two years since their fond farewell on a building-
site in Germany.

This time the scene is Spain's notorious Costa del Crime and
Dennis, Neville, Oz, Barry, Wayne, Moxy and Bomber, still
chronically short of cash and hungry for travel, adventure and
mayhem, rebound from crisis to hilarious crisis.

They and their long-suffering wives and sweethearts find
themselves involved in scrapes that make the old days in
Dusseldorf seem like a dream cruise on the Rhine . . .

HUMOUR/TV TIE-IN   0 7221 36749   £2.75

THE CHILLING NOVEL OF THE ULTIMATE *PSYCHO*-LOGICAL CRIME

from the award winning
WILLIAM BAYER

The two murder victims had little in common – one was a lonely call-girl, the other a prim schoolteacher.

But there was one brutally tantalising connection – their killer had decapitated them both and then switched their heads . . .

"Riveting. It is a novel in which the grit and madness of New York are palpable. It does high honour to the grand tradition of the American psychological thriller." Thomas Keneally

"Very exciting. The plot is impeccable. I recommend it highly." *The Spectator*

0 7221 14958   CRIME   £2.50

A selection of bestsellers from SPHERE

FICTION

HUSBANDS AND LOVERS	Ruth Harris	£2.95 ☐
SWITCH	William Bayer	£2.50 ☐
VITAL SIGNS	Barbara Wood	£2.95 ☐
THE ZURICH NUMBERS	Bill Granger	£2.75 ☐

FILM & TV TIE-INS

BOON	Anthony Masters	£2.50 ☐
LADY JANE	Anthony Smith	£1.95 ☐

NON-FICTION

LET'S FACE IT	Christine Piff	£2.50 ☐
A QUIET YEAR	Derek Tangye	£2.50 ☐
THE 1986 FAMILY WELCOME GUIDE		
	Jill Foster & Malcolm Hamer	£4.95 ☐
THE ABSOLUTELY ESSENTIAL		
GUIDE TO LONDON	David Benedictus	£4.95 ☐

All Sphere books are available at your local bookshop or newsagent, or can be ordered direct from the publisher. Just tick the titles you want and fill in the form below.

Name _____

Address _____

_____

Write to Sphere Books, Cash Sales Department, P.O. Box 11, Falmouth, Cornwall TR10 9EN

Please enclose a cheque or postal order to the value of the cover price plus:

UK: 55p for the first book, 22p for the second book and 14p for each additional book ordered to a maximum charge of £1.75.

OVERSEAS: £1.00 for the first book plus 25p per copy for each additional book.

BFPO & EIRE: 55p for the first book, 22p for the second book plus 14p per copy for the next 7 books, thereafter 8p per book.

Sphere Books reserve the right to show new retail prices on covers which may differ from those previously advertised in the text or elsewhere, and to increase postal rates in accordance with the PO.